THE OXFORD TREASURY OF
Fairy Tales

GERALDINE McCAUGHREAN
SOPHY WILLIAMS

For Daniel Ron – GM

OXFORD
UNIVERSITY PRESS

Great Clarendon Street, Oxford OX2 6DP

Oxford University Press is a department of the University of Oxford.
It furthers the University's objective of excellence in research, scholarship,
and education by publishing worldwide in

Oxford New York

Auckland Bangkok Buenos Aires Cape Town Chennai
Dar es Salaam Delhi Hong Kong Istanbul Karachi Kolkata
Kuala Lumpur Madrid Melbourne Mexico City Mumbai Nairobi
São Paulo Shanghai Taipei Tokyo Toronto

Oxford is a registered trade mark of Oxford University Press
in the UK and in certain other countries

Text © Geraldine McCaughrean 2003
Illustrations © Sophy Williams 2003

The moral rights of the author and artist have been asserted

Database right Oxford University Press (maker)

First published 2003
This edition published in 2012

British Library Cataloguing in Publication Data available

ISBN 978-0-19-279446-8 (Hardback)
ISBN 978-0-19-279445-1 (Paperback)

1 3 5 7 9 10 8 6 4 2

Typeset in Berkley Book
Calligraphy by Stephen Raw

Printed in Thailand

Paper used in the production of this book is a natural,
recyclable product made from wood grown in sustainable forests.
The manufacturing process conforms to the environmental
regulations of the country of origin.

Contents

Sleeping Beauty

As sharp as a needle, the sun broke through and shone on the royal palace. How could the sun not shine, on such a happy day? All the dukes and duchesses were there, all the barons and baronets and countesses. Musicians were playing, chefs cooking, and chroniclers scribbling in their history books:

'Today the Princess Beauty is christened, first and beloved child of the king and queen, heiress to the throne. Never has this kingdom of ours seen such celebrations! Here have come wizards and wise men, and fairies of every colour, all with magical gifts for our baby princess . . .'

But no. Look again. One name is not on the list. The Grey Fairy was not invited. 'She has a tongue as sharp as a needle,' the queen had said, when the guest lists were drawn up. 'Must we invite her?'

So now all colours of fairies but grey stood before the cradle and touched the baby with their glittering wands:

'I give her Love.'

'And I give her Laughter.'

'I give her Beauty.'

'And I give her Health.'

Suddenly, a log in the great fireplace spat, and an ember flew out on to the carpet. Up from the ember sprang the Grey Fairy. 'And I say that before she is full grown, she shall prick her finger at a spinning wheel and DIE!' The fairy hurled her curse into the cradle like a handful of rusty nails, and the baby began to cry.

'No, no!' cried the queen.

'Take that back!' roared the king.

'Please!' begged the assembled guests. But the Grey Fairy only turned to grey smoke and curled away up the chimney.

Only one fairy remained who had not yet given her christening gift. Now, this Lilac Fairy raised her wand in blessing over the screaming baby. 'The Grey curse cannot be lifted—but it can be blunted. My gift to you, Princess Beauty, is this: you shall not die but only sleep until a greater magic than mine can wake you!'

The christening broke up in confusion and panic. Soldiers were sent out through the whole city, through the whole kingdom. 'Destroy all the spinning wheels! Burn them on bonfires!' commanded the king. 'If there are no spinning wheels, she can never prick herself. Hurry! Burn every one! And find the Grey Fairy! Perhaps she can be made to eat her words!'

No trace was found of the Grey Fairy, but spinning wheels by the hundred were smashed and burned, their sharp spindles pulled out like the stings out of wasps. The sheep in the fields went unsheared for want of wheels to spin their wool. But Princess Beauty grew, unharmed, into a toddler, a girl, a young woman.

Naturally, no one spoke to her about the dreadful matter of the Curse, and thanks to the fairy blessings (and her own good nature) she was the sweetest, most beautiful, most loved princess in the history of the nation.

On her sixteenth birthday, Beauty was playing hide-and-seek with her cousins. When it was her turn to hide, she opened a cupboard door and slipped inside. At the back of the cupboard, she noticed a small door. Beyond the door, a staircase, steep and spiral,

wound up past arrow slits and alcoves draped with cobwebs. And there at the top was a turret room she had never known existed before. The door stood open and from inside came the whirra-whirra-whirr of a wheel, spinning.

'Come in, dearie. Have you never seen a spinning wheel? No? It's for twining wool into thread. Come closer and see how it's done.' The spinner was a woman all in grey. Even her hair and face were grey—like something that has lived out of the sunlight too long. But her grey smile was inviting enough. 'Would you like to try, dearie? Just take hold of the spindle . . .'

'Oh! My finger!' Beauty showed the prick to the grey lady, but the spinner only laughed at the drop of blood on her fingertip. Laughed and laughed and laughed.

Beauty ran back to the door, back down the stairs. But her head was swimming, so that the spiral stair seemed to be unwinding under her feet. She stumbled through the cupboard and out into the hall, holding up her finger: 'Mother! Mother, look!' And then the black and white flagstones heaved like the sea, and Beauty felt herself falling, falling, falling . . .

Asleep.

The queen grieved as though her daughter were dead already. She kissed her—over and over—but for all she loved Beauty, hers was not Love's Kiss. Beauty did not wake. 'She may as well be dead,' said the queen bitterly, as Beauty was carried to her bed in the west tower. 'Shall I ever live to see her eyes open again?'

The king did his best to comfort her, but his kiss did not wake Beauty either, and he did not know how long his daughter might sleep.

In Fairyland, all the candles guttered and went out. That was how the fairies knew that the Curse had been fulfilled. Beauty had fallen into her terrible sleep. 'Let us take pity on the king and queen and everyone who loves Beauty,' they said. 'Let all sleep, and not her alone. Let sleep shroud the palace, and magic protect them from harm until Love's Kiss arrives.'

So, one by one, the members of the royal household fell asleep. The guards by the doors, the cooks making supper, the dogs by the fire, the king blowing his nose. Just as sheets are hung over the furniture of an empty house, sleep was thrown over the entire court. The horses in the stables, the doves in the cote fell into a magical sleep, keeping Beauty company on her long dream-journey.

Around the castle, the hedges grew, as unsheared

as the sheep. The flowers in the garden beds ran wild. Briars and brambles rolled in from the forest. Trees grew up from acorn to oak, from conker to horse-chestnut, from stone to plum tree. And the royal rose garden tumbled among the trees, weaving a magical web of thorny suckers no outsider could break through.

Now no one could reach the royal palace. Many tried but turned back. The people of the kingdom were sorry to lose their king and queen and princess, but time eased their sorrow, and they had lives to live. They told their children about the Fairy Curse, but it sounded more like a story than history. And in time the trees grew so tall, the rose thorns so dense, that nothing of the palace could be seen from the highway. Nothing.

*   *   *

One hundred years later, a bee with a sting as sharp as a needle stung the horse of Prince Charmant as he rode along the highway of a foreign kingdom. The horse bolted, and carried the prince off the highway and into a wood. He thought he saw, among the treetops, the gleam of sun shining on a distant window, and tried to ride towards the building. But he found no pathway through the briars and brambles.

A woman sat on a log, stringing lilac flowers into a daisy chain. 'What building is that?' he asked her.

'A castle. There's no road to it. You must cut your way through the briars if you want to reach it. They say there's a princess asleep inside. A very beautiful princess . . .'

Prince Charmant was intrigued. His heart raced a little, at the thought of the beautiful princess. He drew his sword and struck at a thorny bramble. But either his sword was sharper than he knew, or the bramble died at that very moment, for it dropped to the ground at his feet, withered and brown. 'Did you see that?' he said, turning back to the woman. But she had gone. There was no sign of her anywhere.

On and on, hacking and slicing at the dense undergrowth, Prince Charmant forged a path towards the castle. He could see it more clearly now: a turret, a dome . . . It was hard work, but not so hard as he had expected, for the wood seemed to be dying, withering, dropping its autumn leaves on his head like coloured blessings. At last, scratched and panting, he stood on the palace steps listening to a soft purring sound—like a thousand contented cats—coming from inside. He put his ear to the lock. It could not be . . . Yes, it was! It was snoring. The guards in the inner courtyard stood about, back-to-back, snoring and sound asleep!

Charmant leaned his shoulder against the door, and it swung open. There were flowers and flags festooning every wall—as though time had stopped in the middle of a grand celebration. A cake with sixteen candles stood, unnibbled—even the mice in this castle were asleep!—the sixteen candles not yet lit. And everywhere, there were people—strewn untidily about, hats awry, sleeping in heaps on the floors and sofas and stairs.

Charmant climbed over them. A curious sensation of excitement gripped him—as though he was about to make the most important discovery of his life. Something like a strain of music was throbbing inside his head, telling him to go on, to hunt and search, to look for the princess.

'She could be any one of these,' he told himself, as he stepped over a ring of sleeping schoolgirls in party dresses. 'But she is not,' said the music in his head.

He searched the east tower and the chapel. He found the king and queen, she with her face all salty with dried tears, he in the act of blowing his nose. Then Charmant climbed the west tower and came to a bedchamber especially full of flowers. The bed had white damask curtains and the cover was embroidered with intertwining roses.

And there on the pillow he saw a face which stabbed his heart like a needle—the most beautiful face he had ever seen. So deathly white was the princess that he took hold of the hand on the cover, thinking it would

be cold. A drop of blood on the princess's finger smeared his hand, warm and wet.

Then Prince Charmant did something most improper for a prince of the royal blood. He should have waited. He should have asked permission of the king, of the queen, of the girl herself. But he could not help it. Her beauty had worked a kind of magic on his heart. He bent and kissed the sleeping princess on her lips.

Something brushed his face. It was the princess's lashes, a-flicker. 'Look, mother. I pricked my finger,' she murmured, and sat up.

Throughout the palace, dogs scratched, horses stamped, cats stretched. Guards overbalanced, viscounts sneezed, the king blew his nose. The guests picked themselves up off the ballroom floor, and little girls asked if it was time to eat the birthday cake. Noise filled up each room and staircase and hall like a goblet filling with wine.

But up in the white chamber in the west tower, neither Prince Charmant nor Princess Beauty spoke. They just looked at one another in wonder, she a hundred years older than he, yet not a day's difference in the age of their hearts.

'Will you marry me?' he said.

'I suppose I should, now that you've kissed me,' said Beauty. 'But first we'd better finish the game, hadn't we? Whose turn is it to count to fifty?'

Rumpelstiltskin

Fathers like nothing better than to talk about their children—to show them off, to sing their praises. Miller Thumb talked about his daughter all the time. In fact he boasted and bragged and began to embroider the truth.

'My Polly sweeps up the mill every night!' (True.)

'My Poll spins at her wheel every morning!' (True.)

'In fact, my Poll can spin straw on that wheel of hers!' (Unlikely.)

'Yes, yes; in fact, no word of a lie: my Poll can spin straw into gold!' (Oh dear.)

'No!' His friends at the inn were so astonished that one ran and told the lord of the manor; the lord told the king.

'Send your daughter to the palace,' said the letter delivered next day to the mill. 'By order of the King.' Miller Thumb was thrilled. 'He must have heard how pretty you are and wants to marry you!' he said to Polly.

'Don't be foolish, father,' said Polly. 'Kings don't marry country girls.' But she brushed her hair and went to the palace, and the king's eyes flashed with pleasure at the sight of her.

'Come with me,' he said, and with a grip disagreeably tight on her wrist, he led Polly to a small tack-room behind the stables.

Strange place for a spinning wheel, thought Polly.

'I can't abide braggarts,' said the king. 'Spin this bale of straw into gold by morning, or I shall cut off your father's head and put a stop to his boasting.'

The door banged. The bolt shot shut. The horses in the stable next door stamped their hard-shod feet. And Polly wept. 'Oh, father, father, what have you done, and what can I do to put it right? Spin straw into gold? It's never been done in the history of the world, and I'm not the one to do it first!'

'But I am!'

From a bin of bent, discarded horseshoes, a strange old man poked out a poker-long nose. It was as bent as a horseshoe and red as rust. 'I'll do your spinning for you. At a price.'

'What can I give you, except my thanks?' gasped Polly.

'That necklace of yours would do.'

And so the bargain was struck. Polly gave up her necklace, and the little man gave up his night, spinning the wheel till it whistled. Straws twined together, then fell from the spindle like golden woodshavings, curling and coiling on the dirty floor. Long before morning, the straw was all gone, and gold strewings covered the floor. The little spinner climbed back into his barrel, and Polly fell asleep.

When the king opened the door, he stared. 'It was true! The miller was telling the truth!' He was sorry now that he had given Polly only one bale of straw to spin. 'Come with me.' And with a grip disagreeably tight on her arm, he led her to the royal sewing room.

Strange place for a haystack, thought Polly, as men with pitchforks piled twenty bales of straw in the centre of the room.

'Spin all this into gold before morning,' said the king, 'or I'll cut off your father's head—and yours too!' You see, the king was as fond of gold as the miller was of boasting.

The door slammed, the bolt shot shut. The courtiers in the room next door sniggered and shuddered and went away. And Polly wept. 'Oh, father, father, what have you brought me to, and how am I to get myself out of it? Spin straw into gold? I'd need the luck in a barrel of horseshoes to do that!'

'But I wouldn't,' said a voice. Out of the coal scuttle wriggled the

same little man, spilling coals across the turkey rug. 'I'll do your spinning for you. At a price.'

'But what can I give you, except my thanks?'

'That bracelet of yours would do.'

So the bargain was struck. Polly gave up her bracelet, and the little man gave up a day and a night to spinning. The wheel spun so fast that its three feet danced on the floor. The spinner was gone when Polly awoke, and the whole big room was carpeted in shavings of gold.

When the king opened the door, he danced a little caper and beamed. 'No fluke! No trick of the eye! You really can spin straw into gold! Come with me.' And holding her prisoner-tight, for fear she escape him, he led her to the ballroom of the palace. Behind them trotted the prime minister carrying the spinning wheel. Men were pitching bale after bale of straw in through the windows, filling the vast hall from floor to ceiling. 'Spin this into gold by morning, and I shall marry you to my son!' declared the king.

'No, I can't—' Polly began to say.

But the double doors slammed, their bolts shot shut. The king's voice echoed back down the long corridor: 'Then you shall die, girl!'

Polly sat down and wept. 'Oh, father, father, what did I ever do to deserve this? Spin all this straw into gold? It would take all the magic in the land to do it, and I haven't one speck.'

'But I have,' said a voice. Out from amid the stacked

straw, like a hamster emerging from its nest, burrowed the ugly little man, cracking his skilful finger joints. 'I'll spin all this and make you the prince's bride. At a price.'

Polly looked down at her bare arms, touched her bare throat. 'I've nothing but my pinafore and petticoat to give you,' she said.

'Don't want them.'

'A kiss, then.'

'Save it for the prince.'

'My thanks, then. What else?'

'A promise. Promise to give me whatever you hold in your arms on the happiest day of your life, and I'll spin the straw into gold.'

Polly thought of her wedding. Isn't that the happiest day of any girl's life? She thought of the wedding bouquet she would be holding that day, and imagined tossing it to the little goblin.

So the bargain was struck; Polly gave her promise, and the little man gave his all to spin the straw. Gold fell like shavings from a lathe, and the spinning wheel turned so fast that its three little feet wore pits in the polished floor. Its spokes whistled and its hub threw out sparks. But unspun straw still towered over them both in sweet-smelling cliffs.

Just as morning light crept in at the windows—just as the king's steps echoed down the corridor—the last thread of gold trickled from the spindle, and the goblin disappeared in a flash of golden chaff.

When the king opened the double doors, he had never seen so much gold in all his life. He skipped and jumped and clapped his hands. 'Excellent! You shall marry my son and spin gold for him every day of your life!'

Fortunately, the prince had other ideas of married life. 'My bride will never sully her hands with spinning!' he said, caressing Polly's fingers in a most agreeable way. In fact he was a wonderful husband in every respect, and their wedding was the happiest day of Polly's young life. But although she peered around from the church steps, cradling her bouquet, looking for the little spinner, she saw no sign of him—no poker nose, no squint, no long, crackling fingers.

The old king died and the prince became king, Polly his queen.

Polly forgot all about her bargain. She was very happy. In fact her happiness grew every day until, three years later, her baby son was born. Then, cradling him in her arms and gazing at his curling lashes and tiny, perfect hands, Polly realized that wedding days were nothing compared with joy like this.

'I'll take him now,' said a voice. And out from the brand new cradle clambered the spinner, cracking his long, skilful finger joints. 'You swore to give me whatever you were holding in your arms on the happiest day of your life. Here it is, and here am I. Give me the child!'

'No, no!' cried Polly. 'Take anything! Take all I have, but don't take my baby!'

'I want nothing else. I, who can spin straw into gold? What else could I possibly want? All I ever wanted was the child. Now waiting and work have brought round the hour. Hand him over to me! That's the rules of the game.'

'But it's not a game!' cried Polly. 'Or if it is, why did I never have a chance to win? Oh, spinner, spinner, give me a fair chance in an unfair world!'

The spinner gave a hideous cackle and flexed his crackling fingers. 'Very well. I've waited three years. I can wait three days longer. Here's a riddle for you—to make the game fairer:

> *What's my name?*
> *That's the game.*
> *Search about.*
> *Find it out.*
> *If you can,*
> *Keep your wee man.*
> *If you can't,*
> *Then you shan't.*
> *Three times I'll come,*
> *Then playing's done:*
> *I keep your son!'*

Turning a single cartwheel, he disappeared, leaving a smell in the air like rotting straw.

Polly called out the army and had them search the town. They emptied every barrel of horseshoes, every coal scuttle, and pulled apart every hayrick in the realm. The young king offered rewards, and gathered in every church register of christenings. The goblin came back for the first time, and they asked him: 'Is your name Aaron or Bernard, Yves or Zachariah? Is your name Africa or India, Russia or Franz?'

But he only laughed and disappeared in a puff of flour shrieking, 'Guess again! You'll never guess!'

The king posted suggestion boxes on every street corner, and the people (who loved their new king and queen dearly) thought of all the

names they had ever heard. The goblin came back for the second time, and Polly asked him: 'Is your name Horse or Monkey or Lion? Is your name Pixie or Elf or Goblin?'

But the spinner only laughed and disappeared in a sprinkling of crumbs squealing, 'Guess again! You'll never guess!'

In desperation Polly rode the kingdom from end to end, from top to bottom, from the mountains to the sea. She eavesdropped from rooftops, listened at locks, and jotted down names on her cuffs and the palm of her hand. But in her heart of hearts she knew that no one knew the spinner's name except the spinner himself.

She was riding back to the palace, her baby asleep on her back, when the road passed through a forest dark with more than shadow. Far off she saw the glimmer of a fire, and heard a crackling like twigs. Creeping closer, she saw the spinner himself, dancing in a frenzy of joy round the campfire. He was wriggling his long, noisy fingers in the air and singing:

Move every stone, drain every bog;
Ask all the cats and every dog;
Dig up the sea with a single oar:
You won't find what you're looking for!
Search the night with candleshine:
Soon your baby will be mine.
Guess again and lose the game,
For Rumpelstiltskin is my name!'

Polly turned her face to the moon and smiled, then tugged on her reins and quietly rode on through the wood.

Next day, the spinner came for the third and last time, carrying a willow basket under his arm to put the baby in.

'Is your name Avril or Maggie or Sandra?' said Polly. 'Is your name Mars or Venus or Saturn?'

The spinner reached into the royal cradle to tickle the royal baby. 'No, no! Ha ha! I win! I win!'

'Or is it Rumpelstiltskin?' said Polly, and the name crackled on her tongue.

The spinner gave a shriek and his nose uncurled with rage. 'Who told you?! Spies and traitors! Who told you?! I'll cut out their tongues!' Such a temper seized him that he stamped and stamped, feet dancing just where the spinning wheel had danced as it spun straw into gold.

All of a sudden, the floor gave way, and a gaping hole swallowed Rumpelstiltskin like a well swallowing a bent penny. Purple smoke filled the air, and when it cleared there was no trace of the spinner but for that gaping hole and a scream of rage echoing through the palace: 'RUMPELSTILTSKIN!!'

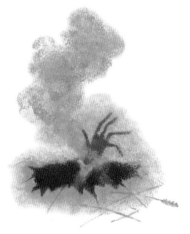

Rapunzel

Once, in the salad days of the world, there was a plant called a bell-flower, or sometimes rapunzel. It was not grown for its pretty bell-shaped flowers but for the root beneath the ground, which made a healthy salad. You probably would not eat it: I'd rather not. But Greta wanted more than anything in the world to eat a plate of rapunzel. She was ill: thin and frail and sickly, and her beauty was withering fast like the flowers of an unrooted plant.

'Gil! Gil!' she whispered to her husband. 'Fetch me bell-flowers, or I shall die before the week is out!'

Unfortunately, the only bell-flowers in the whole county grew in their neighbour Grizzel's garden. And Grizzel was a witch.

Gil loved his wife dearly. He was terribly afraid of the witch, but more afraid of losing his darling Greta. So that night he climbed over the garden wall, picked the bell-flowers and put them in a vase by his wife's bed.

'Where are the roots?' groaned Greta. 'Can I eat flowers, you fool? Bring me the roots!'

So Gil went back next night with a trowel, and treading softly, creeping silently past the belladonna and snapdragons, dug up the roots of the sweet rapunzel.

'Thief! Villain! Vandal!' The witch stood over him, a broom held high, its burning twigs lighting up the garden and his guilty deed. 'You'll pay for this!'

'Anything! I'll pay you anything! My dearest possession! But please let me have some rapunzel, or I'm sure my wife will die!'

'Your dearest possession?' mused Grizzel.

'Name it.'

'Pay when I ask you for payment,' said the witch, suddenly calm and smiling. 'Here are some I picked earlier.' And from under her cloak she took a small basket of roots, clean and ready to eat.

The salad was the best medicine in the world for Greta. At the very sight of it, her face brightened; at the very taste, she felt better. Within a week she was strong and well. Within the year, she was expecting a baby.

It was the prettiest baby, too—fit and beautiful, with lots of golden hair. Greta and her husband would stand for hours in silent wonder, looking down at their first child, their baby daughter.

'We'll call her Bell-flower,' said he.

'Rapunzel, yes,' said she. And Rapunzel was their dearest possession.

'Pay me now as you promised me then!' Suddenly Grizzel stood on the other side of the crib, a moses-basket under her arm and a grin on her wizened face.

'What does she mean, Gil? What does she want?'

'No! You can't take our daughter! Not Rapunzel! No!'

'I've thought of nothing else since I first planted the seed in my garden. Give her over! A promise is a promise, and promises must be kept!'

Neither tears nor pleading would change Grizzel's mind: she had planned this terrible bargain all along. Putting the baby girl in her basket, she flew away, far and farther than far.

Grizzel had always wanted a child. She had always dreamed of having a little daughter all to herself—someone to love her despite her ugly face and nastier nature. So she flew on her broomstick into the deepest forest in the world—to a tower already prepared for her precious prize. Taller than the trees, and without any stairs, the tower stood like a lighthouse in a sea of green, one room at the very top.

And no door.

As the years passed, twining plants climbed the brickwork, almost as high as the single window at the top.

Inside, Rapunzel also grew—from a pretty baby to a beautiful young woman, though there was no mirror for her to look in and realize this. She saw no other human being. Only Grizzel who came and went by the window.

Rapunzel's hair grew as long as the twining plants outside—a glossy hank of shining golden hair. It was Grizzel's pride and joy. It was also very useful.

When her broomstick wore down to a flightless stump, the old witch could still visit her precious prisoner. She would stand at the base of the tower and call:

'Rapunzel! Rapunzel! Let down your golden hair!'

And Rapunzel would let fall her plait, like a rope, for the witch to climb. She loved the witch (who else was there to love?) though she felt an emptiness inside her which she could not understand.

'Is there truly no one else in the world but you and I?' she would ask.

'No one you would want to meet, dearie. No one you need ever meet.'

All day long, Rapunzel was alone—alone and lonely. So she sang, and her voice thrilled the birds for miles around. One day, a young man lost in the wood heard her singing and walked towards the sweet sound. The singing brought him to a clearing, and in the clearing he saw a tower. At the foot of the tower, an old crone was calling: 'Rapunzel! Rapunzel! Let

down your golden hair!' And lo and behold! a beautiful girl came to the window and uncoiled her shining golden plait. The young man hid and watched until he saw Grizzel finish her visit and leave, climbing down the rope of hair. He waited a while, then came out of hiding.

'Rapunzel! Rapunzel! Let down your golden hair!'

Rapunzel was startled. 'Come day, go day,' she said to herself. 'It seems only a moment since Grizzel was here yesterday.' But being a good obedient girl (and very afraid of Grizzel's temper) she let down her plait at once.

Goodness! How heavy the old woman seemed today! How big a breakfast she must have eaten!

Then—one, two—over the windowsill came the hands which should have been old and veined, the hair which should have been grey and thin, the face which should have been ugly and toothless. And they were none of those things! The most beautiful creature Rapunzel had ever seen climbed in through her window.

'Oh!' she said. 'I've seen deer and boar. I've seen weasels and foxes. But what are you?'

'I'm Prince Florian,' said the young man, staring almost as much.

Then they talked and talked. Rapunzel found out the truth about the world, and the prince found out the truth about himself—that he was in love with Rapunzel and wanted to marry her.

'Tomorrow I shall come back for you! Tomorrow, when I've found my way out of this forest. I'll bring a rope for you to climb down and we shall ride away together—to the cities and fields and places you've never seen!'

The emptiness inside Rapunzel was gone. She knew now that Grizzel had lied to her, deceived her, imprisoned her, but she was too full of happiness to be angry. Her lover climbed down her hair, and the forest swallowed him up from sight, but she stayed by the window till the darkness was as thick as tar, watching the way he had gone. Then she fell asleep with her forehead on the sill.

'Rapunzel! Rapunzel! Let down your golden hair!'

Rapunzel started awake. 'So soon? Have you come back so soon, my love?' she said, hurrying to tumble her hair down the tower. 'Quickly! Quick! We must get away from here before Grizzel comes on her daily visit!'

Over the sill—one, two—came veiny hands, grey hair, toothless ugly face. 'So! Have I found you out, little Miss Liar? Have I come too early

for your liking?' The jealousy in Grizzel's face blazed like a furnace. Her treasure, locked up in its treasure chest of stone, had been grasped by other hands, kissed by other lips. A pair of scissors flashed in the sunlight and—SNICK SNACK!–she cut through Rapunzel's lovely hair, cut through the love between them.

Lowering Rapunzel to the ground with her own severed plait, Grizzel screeched after her: 'Go! Get away! See how you fare in the wilderness without me to wait on you hand and foot! Go hungry! Go lonely and unloved! Ungrateful wretch! Go!'

Rapunzel took to her heels and ran, ploughing into the depths of the dangerous forest, at the mercy of weather and wolves and weariness.

But Grizzel's temper was not yet fed.

Grizzel waited for the prince.

'Rapunzel! Rapunzel! Let down your golden hair!' called Prince Florian. Down snaked the shimmering plait. Up and up climbed the prince—above the treetops, up to the little window. Moss fell from under his scrabbling boots.

Suddenly, as he reached the sill, a face loomed out above him, and a pair of veiny, gnarled hands let go the rope of hair. As Florian fell he could hear Grizzel's cackling laugh. 'Thought you'd steal her, did you? My girl? My beauty? Well, you're too late!'

From top to bottom of the tower he fell, entwined in his lover's cut hair. He fell into the brambles, and his eyes were scratched, so that when he dragged himself away into the forest, like a wounded deer, Prince Florian was blinded—dark-blind.

On and on he wandered, hands outstretched, grazing his palms on the rough tree bark. For weeks he walked, dependent on the kindness of peasants and priests for a bite of bread, a drink of water, some shelter from the cold. Stumbling in winter snow, tripping in summer-tangling briars, he asked everyone he met: 'Have you seen a girl with a golden furlong of hair?' But of course no one had seen such a girl, for there was no such girl to see. He did not say he was a prince: who would have believed him? He did not even ask the way to his home or the comfort of his palace. He wanted only to find Rapunzel.

Then one day—one fine spring morning it was—he heard singing, and he followed the sound to a ramshackle hut in the midst of a stony garden. He could smell the scent of bell-flowers and hear washing flapping in the wind.

Then Prince Florian opened his mouth and joined in the singing of Rapunzel's song, and she heard him and came running.

Ragged and thin and blind, he looked such a piteous sight that Rapunzel thought her heart would break with pity and love. She took him in her arms and wept great tears of regret.

And the tears splashed his eyes—magic tears on a magic morning— and Prince Florian blinked once, blinked twice and saw his dear Rapunzel's face. She no longer had a golden furlong of hair, but then it was not her hair he had loved—not even her beauty. Like the bell-flower, her worth lay deeper down, sweet and healthful: the perfect makings of a princess and a wife.

The Flower of Love

Only one more day and we shall be married!' said Jim to Jemima. 'What man was ever as happy as I!'

'What girl was ever as happy as I?' said Jemima, and rested her head fondly on his shoulder.

They went for a walk in the wood—a last walk before their wedding day. And so entranced were they with each other's company that they walked deeper into the wood than ever before.

'They say there's a castle somewhere in these woods,' said Jim. 'A castle where an old witch lives.'

'Why would anyone build a castle in a wood?' said Jemima. 'Castles are built in the open, on the tops of hills.'

'Ah, but they say this old witch has terrible secrets to hide—prisoners, captives, pretty girls like you,' he teased. Jim could feel her hand trembling deliciously inside his own. 'They say she has taken seven hundred into that castle of hers, and not a one has ever come out again!' and he laughed at the silliness of the story. Jemima's hand slipped from his own, and he turned to see why.

The laugh froze on his lips, for there was no Jemima beside him now—

only a fluttering bluebird buffeting its little fragile body against his arm and shoulder and face. It sang the saddest song a bird ever sang.

Jim would have taken the bluebird in his palm and stroked her feathery little head, but he found he was frozen to the spot—powerless to move! His limbs were as heavy as the branches of the trees round about, his legs fixed as fast as the treeroots. In her distress, Jemima clamoured up against her motionless sweetheart, thrilling shrilly in his ear, but Jim could say nothing to comfort her, do nothing to help her.

Beyond her fluttering wings, he glimpsed a stark iron gateway in an ancient wall. Through it now came a bent old woman, rubbing her bony hands together with glee. 'Another little birdie for me? Good, good. Excellent. Very pretty. Here, my little chickadee. Here, my pretty wee creature.'

'Fly! Fly!' Jim wanted to say, but Jemima was too busy fluttering frantically against his face, trying to rouse him. The witch scurried up, birdcage in hand and, with a dreadful, cackling laugh, scooped little Jemima into the wicker prison.

'Another for my aviary!' she crowed, then snapping her fingers scornfully under Jim's nose, she turned and went back through the gate.

The rain rained on Jim, the wind blew on him and carried away his hat and neckerchief. Not until the sun rose next morning was he able to move again, to rattle at the locked gates, to pound with his fists on the high walls, calling, 'Let her go! Please let her go! She's my all! She's my everything! Jemima!'

Guests gathered for the wedding, but no bride came to church, no bridegroom either. For on his wedding day, Jim was running distractedly round the endless castle wall, trying to find a way in. At last, exhausted and half mad with despair, he went home. Hoping he might wake to find it all a nightmarish dream, he threw himself on his bed and went to sleep.

He dreamed that night that he lay dead and buried under the ground. Out of his heart, bursting through flesh and soil, stones and slab, a small red flower pushed its way up into the sunshine. Its petals brushed the walls of a grim, gloomy castle, and the castle stumbled, tumbled, crumbled to ash. In his dream, Jim snatched the flower and tried to smell its perfume. But the scarlet petals turned to Jemima's face between his hands, and her scarlet mouth called, 'Find me, Jim! Find the Flower of Love! Save me!'

He woke with empty arms, her name on his lips, and he knew that if he could find that Flower, he would be able to enter the Castle of Birds.

He searched the cornfields, but though the poppies were scarlet, they were not the Flower of Love. He searched the meadows, but though he found speedwell and harebells, campanula and foxgloves, he could not find the Flower of Love. He searched the mountainside, but though he found

brave little flowers clinging to the bare rock through drought and rain, none were the flower in his dream. He searched gardens, but though he found forget-me-nots and love-lies-bleeding, he did not find the Flower of Love.

At last, where land meets sea, and east meets west, where high meets low, and diving birds meet flying fish, he spotted a single flower growing from a sheer cliff face. With no thought for his safety—reckless with desperate hope—he climbed the cliff. Skuas wheeled around him, the wind cracked his hair in his eyes. And when he reached it, the Flower of Love had three petals, a stem of thorns and roots as deep as the earth's core.

'O Flower of Love, let me pick you or let me fall into the ocean now and be lost!' he begged. 'Without Jemima, life is nothing to me.' As his fingers closed around the stem, the thorns withdrew, and the Flower of Love broke off as easily as a buttercup. It had given itself to him. Jim fastened it in his buttonhole, and climbed on up to the top of the cliff.

Back in the forest, the shadows did not seem so dark any more. When Jim reached the spot where the magic had paralysed him, no magic seized him and he was able to reach the castle gates unseen. At a touch of the Flower of Love, the gate crumbled to rusty dust, and Jim forged on up the winding driveway, through a maze of black-leafed shrubs, right to the castle door.

With the Flower of Love in his grasp, there was not a lock or bolt which could bar his way, and he was soon inside, climbing spiral staircases, feeling his way along dark, narrow corridors towards the distant twitter of birdsong.

At last he came to a string of rooms, one after another, crammed with shrieking, trilling birds. Tens and dozens of wicker cages hung from the ceiling, each one trembling with the violent flutter of the little bird inside. There were lyre birds, birds of paradise, macaws and canaries, owls and swallows. Orioles and blackbirds sang brilliant, thrilling songs, but all so sad, so heartbreakingly sad, beaks straining between the bars of their cages. The noise, in so small a space, was earsplitting. Jim whirled round and round, his hands over his ears, setting the cages swinging and bumping as he called, 'Jemima! Where are you? How shall I find you among all these?'

'That's right!' said a voice behind him. 'Call till your heart breaks. How will you ever find her among so many? Here are seven hundred of my little pets. Which one is your Jemima, eh? Now, by all the magic at my command, I command you: Stand still!'

Jim froze to the spot, moving neither hand nor head, neither lip nor eyelid. The witch gave a terrible cackle and skipped about among her cages. 'See, my pretty ones? I've caught an intruder. How did he get in, eh? A miracle! How will he get out, eh? An impossibility! Come, little Jemima, come and sing a last song to your foolish, reckless sweetheart before I turn him into a dog or a beetle or a worm!' And she lifted down one of the cages—one with a bluebird inside.

But bringing it close, to wag in Jim's face, she gave a sudden terrible cry and dropped the cage. For she had seen the scarlet flower in Jim's fingers, and the smile on his lips. He was not ensnared by her magic at all!

Out darted his hand and he struck the witch in the face with the Flower of Love. Pollen dusted her crooked nose. Her magical powers fell from her like leaves from a tree in autumn, and the Castle of Birds shook to its very foundations.

Quickly, Jim thrust the flower through the bars of the bluebird's cage, and brushed the pretty feathers with the scarlet petals. And there stood Jemima, her head thrown back in rapturous song! Moments later, twenty and thirty more maidens were dancing around Jim, thanking him, blessing him, as he moved from cage to cage, breaking the enchantment.

Clutching her moth-eaten shawl around her, the Witch of Birds scuttled like a rat towards the stairs.

'Quick! Stop her! She'll get away!' cried Jemima.

'Let her go,' said Jim softly. 'Her magic is all gone. Wherever she runs in the world, the birds of the air will mob her and people will shut their doors against her.' With the Flower of Love in his hand, Jim was powerless to hate even the witch.

People say there was never a man and wife so happy as Jim and Jemima, and they put it down to the couple's great good luck. After all, not many newly-weds come by a castle to live in and a witch's treasure chest to make them rich. But I say it had less to do with castles and treasure than with what Jim and Jemima kept under their pillow. A little scarlet flower which never withered.

Cinderella

Cinderella was not her name. Once, long before, she had had another name. But her stepmother had forgotten it, along with her promise to Cinderella's father. Stepmother had promised, as he lay dying, to love his little daughter as much as she loved her own three, to treat her as kindly as she treated her own three, to share his money evenly between all four girls. But he was no sooner dead than the promise was forgotten. His daughter was turned out of her bedroom and made to sleep in the scullery, to clean the house and do the laundry, to cook and wash up and fetch in the coal. From dawn till dead of night, she had to work, to make life comfortable for Stepmother and her three lazy stepsisters, Raviola, Rigatona, and Linguina. No money was squandered on new clothes for her, no good food wasted on her. So her old clothes wore out into threadbare shreds. Then they called her Cinderella, because she slept among the cinders of the kitchen fire to keep warm.

But there was one thing Cinderella had which her stepsisters could not take away: her beauty. Their faces were like three plates of meatballs, but hers was as lovely as a bowl of creamed strawberries. They were as

big and bulky as barrels and trunks and crates; she was as slender as a quiver.

Sometimes Cinderella wished she were not so pretty, for it made the sisters spiteful with jealousy. But mostly Cinderella wished for gentleness—for a smile, for a kind word, for someone to look her way without snarling a command:

'Scrub the steps, Cinderella!'

'Mend my shoes, Cinderella!'

'Wash my curtains, Cinderella!'

'Make my supper!'

Cinderella never complained. She was as sweet-natured as she was beautiful, and even they, with their bullying cruelty, could not stop her dreaming her happy daydreams.

One day, a letter was delivered to the door by a footman in a scarlet jacket. It was an invitation to a ball—to the Royal Ball. Up and down the street, windows were flying open, people were calling out to their neighbours:

'Did you get one?'

'Everybody got one! The king's invited everyone!'

'Every unmarried girl, anyway!'

'He wants Prince Boniface to choose himself a wife!'

Raviola, Rigatona, and Linguina twitched like hamsters at the sound of that word—'Wife'. This was what Fate had been saving up for them: marriage to a prince—riches, fame, luxury for the rest of their days. Each vain sister thought the same thing: he's bound to choose me! Each sister looked at her other two sisters and writhed with delight and hatred.

'You're so ugly, Raviola, the prince will never choose you!'

'You're so fat, Rigatona, he'll never choose you.'

'You're so stupid, Linguina, no one will ever choose you!'

They never even thought to look at Cinderella. Only their mother had the wit to know: pretty Cinderella must not be allowed to go to the ball.

Soon the day of the ball arrived. Stepmother kept Cinderella busy filling baths, fetching dresses, buying ribbons, cleaning shoes ... Raviola, Rigatona, and Linguina were in a frenzy to look their best, primping and prancing in front of the mirror, trying on one dress, trying on another. They painted their mouths, painted their cheeks; they even painted their eyebrows and coloured their hair. At last, when they stood in the hall on the evening of the ball, they looked quite ready for

Christmas: a goose, a turkey, and a pork roast all trussed and larded.

'May I get ready now?' asked Cinderella, fetching them their velvet cloaks.

'YOU?!' Her stepsisters shrieked and twittered in horror.

'You?' said her stepmother, with a calm and chilling laugh. 'Do you really suppose the king wants a scullery maid eating off his best china?'

So saying, she swept her three daughters ahead of her out of the door and locked it loudly behind her. The sound of their carriage rattling away was almost drowned out by the three stepsisters squabbling and bickering:

'He'll marry me!'

'No, me!'

'No, me!'

Cinderella caught sight of herself in the hall mirror. Had she really thought to go to the ball? That unwashed, white-faced, half-starved waif in the mirror? Just because every young woman in the city was invited? Had she really thought her stepmother would grant her one glorious, happy night? Tears crawled like woodlice down Cinderella's grimy face, and she sank down just where she was, on the hall rug, hugging her knees, rocking to and fro. The seventeen clocks in the silent house ticked like clicking tongues: TICK TOCK TUT TUT TUT.

As the hall clock struck eight, the front door—the locked front door—swung open and in came a small, elderly woman, along with a flurry of dead leaves. She leaned on a silver-topped cane. 'Why are you crying, Cinderella?'

'Oh, it's stupid. I'm silly. Oh, but I did so want to go to the ball!' sobbed Cinderella, trying to dry her eyes on her apron.

'And so you shall, my dear. But jump up. There's work to do and it won't get done by sitting on the rug!'

Cinderella wondered if she was dreaming. But she got up and did exactly as the old lady said—'Wash your face. Comb your hair.'—It was easy: she was used to doing what she was told. 'Fetch me six mice from the traps, and a pumpkin from the garden.' It was soon done: she was used to heavy work and dirty, unpleasant jobs. 'Now set them down out there, in the road.'

The night was cold. The distant palace blazed with lights. Cinderella would have liked to stand and stare, imagining the dancing. But the little old lady chivvied her on: 'Hurry, hurry. Don't keep him waiting!'

'Who? Keep who waiting?' said Cinderella.

'Well, the prince, of course!'

'Oh, but I—Look, I don't mean to be rude, but who are you, exactly?'

The old lady raised her silver-topped cane and flourished it three times in the air. There in the street, where the pumpkin and six mice had stood, a glass coach drawn by six white horses glittered in the starlight. 'I'm your fairy godmother, of course, child. Now hurry! The orchestra is just tuning up.'

'But I can't—' Cinderella began. 'A scullery maid can't . . .' Then she caught sight of herself in a puddle of rain. She was wearing a dress of white organza sprinkled with silver flowers. Her petticoats were of gold lace, and her hair was plaited with lilies. On her feet were glass slippers with heels like the stems of wineglasses, but so comfortable that she only noticed them as she climbed into the coach.

'One thing you must remember, child. On the strike of midnight, all magic fails and falters. Even mine. Be home by midnight, my dear, or you may never get home at all . . . Oh, my! Your dear father would be so proud of you tonight!'

'Did you know him, then? Did he send you?'

But the coach was already moving, the white horses leaping into a gallop without driver or whip. The little old lady standing on the road grew smaller and smaller in the distance, until she seemed small enough to have stood on the palm of Cinderella's hand.

At the palace, a marble staircase ran down like a white waterfall to the polished dance floor. Heralds blew fanfares to welcome each guest. Raviola, Rigatona, and Linguina were

already dancing, with soldiers of the Royal Guard, but their eyes stayed fixed on the prince, ready to wave or smile or wink if he glanced their way. The prince was not dancing. He looked sad.

'Cheer up, m'lad!' said the king, slapping him on the back. 'Plenty of handsome gals to choose from!'

'I just think it's a poor way to choose a wife,' muttered Prince Boniface. 'I mean, what can I tell, just by dancing with a girl? How can I get to know a girl in one evening?'

A last, late fanfare blew for one last, late arrival, and down the marble stairs came a girl in white organza, sprinkled and plaited with flowers. The dancers on the floor looked up and gasped. Such a dress! Such petticoats! Such shoes!

But the prince saw none of that. He saw the blue of Cinderella's eyes, her shy smile, her quick, skipping feet on the stairs. Hurrying to meet her, he begged her to dance her first dance with him.

''Snot fair, Mummy,' snivelled Raviola. 'They didn't say princesses was going to be here.'

'Who is she, Mummy?' snarled Rigatona. 'I could look like her if you just bought me dresses like that!'

'Do something, Mummy,' whined Linguina. 'He's not even looking our way!'

But for all her burning ambition, there was nothing their mother could do. Prince Boniface had laid eyes on the love of his life, and now no one else existed for him in the whole room.

They danced every dance together; they talked about everything in the world—except who Cinderella was and how she came to be there. Let him mistake her for a princess, she thought, otherwise he might wipe his hands on his jacket and turn away.

She saw her stepsisters, perched like plump cushions on the gilt chairs, sulking. She saw her stepmother scowling and scowling and cramming sweetmeats into her angry mouth. But they did not recognize her—did not see through her disguise, see through her magic-till-midnight finery.

Midnight! Oh!

The clock started to strike. ONE TWO.

'What time is it?' Cinderella gasped. 'Eleven o'clock?'

'Twelve,' said the prince. 'But we have the whole night ahead of us!'

THREE FOUR

'Let me go!'

'Why? Whatever's the matter?'

FIVE SIX

'I have to go! I must!' Cinderella broke away from him and started up the marble stairs.

SEVEN EIGHT

Her legs were weary from dancing. The stairs seemed like a cliff. The prince called out behind her: 'Wait! You've dropped . . .' But she did not, could not wait.

NINE TEN

The cold night air broke over her like a seawave, unplaiting her hair. The six white horses were tossing their heads and pawing the ground, rocking the glass coach.

ELEVEN

As she sped away into the black of night—TWELVE—the coach burst apart around her like a snowball hitting a wall, and she went somersaulting over and over into a ditch. A pumpkin rolled in on top of her. Reaching to gather up her lovely skirts, she found no organza dress, no petticoats of gold . . . though on her left foot she still wore a single glass slipper, as if midnight had taken pity and spared her one shred of her happy, perfect evening.

By the time the three stepsisters and their mother arrived home at dawn, Cinderella was asleep in her usual place, among the embers of the kitchen fire.

'Lazy, idle, good-for-nothing girl!' shrilled Rigatona. 'Get up and make me some breakfast. I've been dancing with the prince all night.'

'Liar!' snivelled Linguina. 'You didn't dance with him once. None of us did. We didn't stand a chance once he had seen that princess woman.'

'Quiet!' snapped their mother. 'She ran away, didn't she? The game's not lost yet. How can he marry a girl who isn't there?'

But next morning, the streets were noisy again with excitement. There were proclamations nailed to every tree, announcing that Prince Boniface had already decided on a wife. He would marry the girl with whom he had danced at the ball, and he would marry no other. Apparently, the lady had left behind, on the steps of the palace, a single glass slipper, and the prince had vowed to find the owner of that slipper. It would be carried from house to house, and every woman in the kingdom must try it on. Thus he would seek her out, hunt her down, the mysterious girl too shy to give him her name.

Raviola, Rigatona, and Linguina broke into howls of misery and rage, and beat on the breakfast table with their fists and foreheads. "Snot fair, Mummy! 'Snot fair!'

'Be quiet, you fools,' snapped their mother, her face set in grim determination. 'Cinderella! Fetch six buckets of ice from the ice-house! Be quick! If the prince wants a foot to fit his precious glass slipper, then that's what he shall have. We'll show him eight of the most delicate feet in Christendom!'

All morning they sat—stepmother and stepsisters—with their feet in buckets of ice. Though the girls whimpered and grizzled and complained—'So co-o-o-old, Mummy!'—and turned quite blue, their mother only glared and told Cinderella to fetch more ice. The cold would make their feet smaller, she said, three sizes smaller.

At last there was a knock at the door. The footman in the scarlet jacket stood once again on the step. This time he carried a crimson cushion and on it the single glass slipper. Pushing the buckets out of sight under the table, the four hobbled to the door. 'Come in! Come in!' said Raviola dragging him into the hall.

'Ah, you've brought back my slipper. So kind,' said Rigatona.

''Snot yours, it's mine. Let me try it on first!' shrieked Linguina.

While they squabbled, their mother calmly took hold of the glass slipper and tried to squeeze her own ice-cold foot into it. But try as she might—try as Raviola and Rigatona and Linguina might—all four had feet like shire horses. The cold had shrunk them, but not enough—not nearly enough to fit the tiny, magical glass slipper.

'Are you all the ladies in the house?' asked the flunkey.

'Yes, yes. Get out of here,' spat Stepmother in a frenzy of disappointment.

'Might I—' said Cinderella, peeping round the kitchen door.

'No! Certainly not! Get back to your work, impudent ragamuffin!' said Stepmother.

'My orders are,' said the flunkey, glimpsing a pretty face at last, 'that every lady in the land—'

'She's no lady. She's the scullery maid!' cried Stepmother and laughed shrilly at the absurd idea of Cinderella trying on the slipper. 'She never even went to the ball! I know! I locked the door on her myself.'

'Even so . . .' said Cinderella, 'I should like to try on the shoe.'

And so she did. It fitted perfectly.

'Absurd! Ridiculous! She obviously wants to trick the prince into marrying her!' bayed Stepmother. 'She's had her feet in ice water to shrink them!'

But when Cinderella pulled from her apron pocket the matching glass slipper, its heel as fine as the stem of a wineglass, the flunkey blushed as red as his jacket and dropped to one knee. 'Begging your pardon, miss, but did you mean to break the prince's heart, running off like that?'

'If I had stayed, he would have found out who I was—what I was, I mean,' said Cinderella looking down at her rags.

'Begging your pardon, miss, but he knew that already. He knew you were the love of his life, and what else matters?'

Cinderella laughed shyly and kissed the flunkey on his bald, shiny head. 'If the prince's heart is broken, tell him I will gladly mend it for him,' she said.

And so she did. Cinderella and Prince Boniface were married within the week, and the wedding party went on for three days—three days of dancing and feasting, three days of music and fireworks. Even Raviola and Rigatona and Linguina enjoyed themselves.

Only their mother stayed at home, behind locked doors, and fumed like an old black cauldron as she stared into the embers of the kitchen fire.

As for Cinderella, she lived happily ever after, just as her father had always meant her to do when, at her birth, he named her. Not 'Cinderella', but Joy.

The Dancing Princesses

It was a time of war. Men thought only of fighting, and girls, left alone and afraid, wanted only to dance their worries away. The King of Terpsichoria did not want his twelve daughters to dance. He valued them like gold and silver and diamonds, and like gold and silver and diamonds he meant to keep them under lock and key where no one else could lay hands on them. So each night he locked them into their bedroom and each morning he found them sleeping there: still his.

But the king was baffled. The king was bewildered. The king was mystified. Every morning, at the foot of the twelve beds, were twelve pairs of satin slippers worn into holes. Twelve times he bought them new dancing slippers. Twelve times twelve! And twelve times twelve times the slippers were worn out overnight—as if the princesses had danced every hour that they slept. The king was baffled. The king was bewildered. The king was mystified. He made a decree:

> *'Let it be known that the king will give in marriage*
> *the hand of a royal princess to the man who can solve*
> *the mystery of the worn slippers!'*

Every man in the land came running to the palace gates.
'I'll solve it!'
'I will!'
'I will!'
The king went on:

> *'Three nights the man may spend in the bedroom*
> *of the princesses. But if after the third night he has*
> *not solved the mystery, he shall die!'*

By the time he had said this, the queue had gone from in front of the palace gates. The princesses were beautiful, but not so beautiful that men would die to have them. War teaches people to cling on tight to their lives.

A few gallant princes came from foreign parts to attempt the quest; to discover the secret. But after three nights, none had even managed to stay awake, let alone find out how the princesses wore out their slippers. And so the princes died.

The princesses would not tell. What did they care if the princes who came never went home again?

Outside town, a wounded soldier sat with his back to a tree and wondered why the war had left him, Musgrave, alive. It had left him no

home, no job, and nothing to eat. So why had it spared his life? To sit in a wood with his back to a tree?

'I suppose you're on your way to the palace to solve the mystery?' An old woman, as wrinkled and brown as a fallen leaf, sat down beside him.

'What palace? What mystery?' said Musgrave. So the old woman told him. 'Why not? I've nothing to lose and everything to gain. I'll give it a try,' said Musgrave.

'Well said. Take this cloak,' said the crone, 'and take some advice, too. When the princesses offer you wine, don't drink it.'

'No one offers a wounded soldier a cup of wine in these heartless times, Granny,' said Musgrave, but he took the dirty rag she thrust into his hands, not wanting to offend her. The cloak looked none too clean, but then neither did Musgrave . . .

The king did not want this common, grubby soldier sleeping in his daughters' bedroom. But there were no princes left, and a hundred more pairs of slippers had been worn to holes since the challenge. So he let Musgrave try, comforting himself that in three days the impertinent young man would be dead like all the rest.

No sooner was Musgrave introduced to the

princesses, than they offered him a cup of wine, rich and red. 'Drink it! Do! You must be so thirsty after all that fighting.' Musgrave wanted it (more than any prince would have done), but he remembered what the old woman had said, and only pretended to drink, letting the luscious wine trickle out of his mouth onto his red jacket. (The stain did not show among all the others.) They showed him to a bed—soft and white and inviting. But many was the night Musgrave had had to stay awake on guard when he was dropping with fatigue. So he laid his head on the pillow, but he only pretended to sleep.

'Poor fool,' said the oldest princess. 'He hardly needed the drugged wine to make him sleep . . . Now! On with your slippers, sisters! Our partners are waiting!'

Eleven princesses leapt out of bed and ran to the great wardrobe where their dresses were kept. But the last little princess was slow to dress. 'So many young men are dead because of our dancing. Must this one die too? All is not well. My slippers are cold tonight.'

But her sisters only laughed at her and rustled into their gowns. Decking their hair and throats with jewels, they gathered together their huge skirts and squeezed into the wardrobe—and out again on the other side, into a secret passageway. A bitter draught spilled from the wardrobe into the room, making Musgrave shiver.

Wrapping himself round in the dirty rag of a cloak, he found, to his alarm, that his body suddenly disappeared! In a panic he clutched at his legs, at his arms. Phew! Still there. He was simply invisible.

Invisible! That meant he could follow the princesses! Creeping through the wardrobe, he closed the door behind him, click.

'What was that?' said the youngest princess. 'All is not well tonight. I feel it in my satins.'

But her sisters only laughed at her and ran on. The tunnel came out into an underground orchard whose trees glimmered with golden leaves. But the princesses did not stop there to dance. They ran on into an orchard whose trees scintillated with silver blossoms. But they did not stop there either to dance. They ran on into an orchard whose trees sparkled with fruits of diamond. Musgrave could not help but catch his breath at so many wonders.

'Who's there?' gasped the youngest princess. 'All is not well tonight. I feel it in my blood.'

But the sisters only laughed at her and ran on across the drawbridge of a subterranean castle. There, twelve princes with eyes of fire and hair of fur and suits of glistening jet took the princesses in their arms and danced with them till morning.

'So that is your secret, is it?' whispered Musgrave to himself.

'Who spoke?' said the youngest princess. 'All is not well tonight: I feel it in my hair!' But her partner only laughed at her and whirled her faster in the dance. The sulphur-yellow walls of the ballroom were lit with flickering red, and the flowers in the vases were not fresh but made of glass.

All night Musgrave watched. Then he followed the twelve princesses back through the three orchards and the tunnel, to their bedroom. Their slippers were worn to holes and they were pale with weariness. Musgrave could have gone then, and hammered on the king's door and told him the secret of the dancing princesses. But instead he ate the breakfast

sent to him—and the lunch and dinner, too, and prepared for a second
night in the bedroom of the twelve princesses.

Again he pretended to drink the wine they gave him. Again he
pretended to sleep. Again the girls got up and crept, giggling and
whispering, through their secret passage to their secret rendezvous.
Again Musgrave followed. Although there was no sky overhead, the way
was not dark, because of the shining of gold leaves, silver twigs, and
fruits of diamond. All night Musgrave watched as the princesses wore
their slippers to shreds dancing, then he followed them back to their
beds.

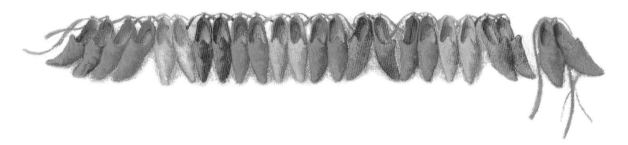

He could have gone then, and demanded to see the king, and claimed
his reward for solving the mystery. But instead he ate the breakfast sent
to him—and the lunch and dinner, too, and prepared for a third night.

On the third night he grew bolder. He followed the princesses so
closely that he stepped on the train of the youngest's dress; she cried out
in fright. Invisible in his magic cloak, Musgrave even joined in the
dancing, tripping the princes with their hair of fur and their jet black
suits, twirling the youngest princess around in his arms.

'Oh! Who touched me?' she said. 'All is not well tonight. I felt it in my arms—the ghost of one of those poor young men we have sent to their deaths!'

But her sisters and the princes laughed at her, and caught hold of her hands, and pulled her into their circle dance.

Back in their bedroom, the princesses kicked off their ragged slippers and fell on their beds, weary past words. The youngest looked with regret at the sleeping soldier in the corner and remembered that today was his day to die. But she too was powerless to stay awake. The nightly dancing was stealing away her strength, stealing away the roses in her cheeks, stealing away her soul . . .

'Speak, soldier. Have you solved the mystery of the worn slippers?' asked the king, expecting to hear the same excuses: 'Please, Your Majesty, I could not stay awake. I tried—I really tried! Spare me my life!'

But Musgrave did not plead for his life. 'I have indeed solved the mystery, Your Majesty,' he said. 'Each night your daughters rise up from their beds and pass through a tunnel to an underground castle where they dance all night and every night with twelve princes. On the way, they pass through an orchard of golden trees, an orchard of silver trees, and an orchard of trees whose fruits are diamonds, to reach a castle with walls of sulphur-yellow and flowers of glass.'

'Lies! All lies!' said the oldest princess, choking down her amazement. 'He is making it all up to save his skin! Tell the liar to prove it!'

So the king went to the daughters' bedroom; so did Musgrave, and so did the executioner, busily sharpening his axe. The king blundered about among the satin dresses and silken petticoats, but could find no tunnel beyond the wardrobe. All he found were twelve pairs of ragged slippers with holes in their soles.

'The man was lying,' sighed the king. 'Take him away, executioner.'

Musgrave put his hand inside his jacket. You may think he pulled out the cloak and disappeared. No. He pulled out instead a leaf of gold, a twig of silver, and a huge diamond shaped like a pear. 'These I picked in the three orchards,' he said. 'And this glass flower I took from a vase in the underground castle.'

Then the princesses burst into tears, knowing that their dancing days were over and they would see no more of the twelve princes. 'Choose your bride,' said the king. 'Choose the oldest and in time you shall inherit my kingdom and rule in my place.'

But Musgrave did not choose the oldest. He chose the youngest. 'I believe she has a little heart left to love me,' he said. 'The others have worn too many holes in their souls.'

And because the king liked Musgrave's answer, and loved his youngest daughter best of the twelve, he shared his kingdom with the soldier anyway.

Which set Musgrave dancing until he wore his old army boots right through to his socks.

The Three Gifts of the North Wind

Times were hard—harder than the dry bread on Jack's table. There was nothing left in the larder but a slab of cheese, nothing in the jug but a swig of milk, no fuel to burn but the chair leg already crackling in the grate. And there wasn't a penny to buy more. But suddenly, with a roar that rattled the chimney, the North Wind blew over the hill, circled the cottage three times and, without even knocking, blustered into the kitchen.

It blew out the fire, spilled the jug of milk, and set the larder door banging. And when it swept out again, there was not a morsel of cheese in the larder, not a bite of bread on the table.

'Oho, very fine, very fine, I'm sure!' said Jack. 'Can't he pick on someone his own size?' And he was so angry that he put on his coat and went after the Wind.

Over the hill he went and through the woods. (He could see which way the Wind had gone, because the corn on the hill and the trees in the wood were laid flat.) Over the river he went and over the sea. (He could judge the course the Wind had steered, because there was wreckage on the waves and fish cast up on the rocks.) Over the horizon

and under the rainbow went Jack, till he came to the home of the North Wind.

'All honour to your Mightiness, and all respect to your fame,' said Jack, 'but what is the world coming to when the strong steal from the weak? Give us back our supper, or my poor old mother will starve!'

The North Wind looked Jack up and down, down and up. 'The supper's eaten. Sometimes I am rash and sudden. I'm sorry.'

'Sorry won't feed my old mother,' said Jack, fists on hips.

'No, but this will,' said the North Wind. And he gave Jack a cow out of his own larder.

Now a cow is a very fair exchange for a meal of bread and cheese—especially since this cow was magic. When she was milked she gave not cream but a stream of gold coins. So Jack happily took the cow and led her homewards.

It was a long journey, so Jack had to spend the night at an inn. When the innkeeper asked him to pay for his supper, Jack simply held a tankard under the cow and milked her. Three gold coins jingled into the mug.

If the innkeeper was startled, he did not show it. 'That's a fine animal you've got there,' he said, and showed Jack to his bed.

But after Jack had gone, that innkeeper danced a jig on the floor, then went and hid Jack's cow in his own barn. In its place he led in a bull, painted it to look just

like Jack's cow, and left it tied up in the same place, saying, 'The lad's a fool, and riches are wasted on a fool.'

So when Jack got home with his 'magic cow', he said, 'Mother, mother, the North Wind gave me a cow that gives gold in place of milk!'

Well, when Jack's old mother tried to milk the cow, she got neither milk nor gold, but a large hole in her cottage wall where the bull ran off. 'Oh, Jack, Jack, you're a gullible fool and I pity any wife that's fool enough to marry you,' said Jack's mother. But he did not hear; he had already gone . . . back to the home of the North Wind.

'All glory to your Mightiness and all sparkle to your fame,' said Jack, 'but what is the world coming to when the wise lie to the trusting? That cow gave gold once and never again. She won't save my old mother from going hungry!'

'I'm puzzled,' said the North Wind.

'Puzzled won't feed my old mother,' said Jack, fists on hips.

'No, but this will,' said the Wind. And he fetched a tablecloth out of his own linen basket, flicking it clean of crumbs.

Now a tablecloth may seem a poor exchange for a cow or a supper. But this cloth was magic. As soon as it was laid flat, and heard the words, 'Feed me food,' it filled up with all manner of wonderful things to eat. So Jack happily took the cloth and headed home.

Once again he stayed overnight at the inn. But this time he ordered no supper. Instead, he laid the cloth on the table, said, 'Feed me food!' and—yum! yum!—there were pies and cold joints, tarts and fruit, jellies and bottles of wine enough to satisfy every hungry traveller in the inn.

If the innkeeper was surprised, he did not show it. But after Jack had gone to bed, he and his wife danced a jig on the messy tables, then fetched out the oldest pillowcase in the house. They stole Jack's magic cloth from under his snoring head, and put the pillowcase there instead, saying, 'The lad's a fool and fools don't deserve feasts.'

So when Jack reached home with his 'magic cloth', and spread it in front of his old mother saying, 'Feed us food,' nothing more nutritious than a bedbug and a flea appeared in front of them.

'Oh, Jack, Jack, you're a fool and a daydreamer, and I

pity the wife that's fool enough to marry you,' said Jack's mother. But Jack did not hear: he had already gone . . . back to the home of the North Wind.

'Long life to your Mightiness and regards to your little ones, but what is the world coming to when the clever play tricks on the foolish? That cloth shrank to the size of a pillowcase before I even got it home, and my poor old mother hasn't had one bite to eat off it.'

'Ah, I think I understand!' said the North Wind.

'So do I,' said Jack (who was not the fool he looked). 'I was robbed by that fat blighter of an innkeeper. But what can I do about it?'

'Take this bag,' said the North Wind, 'and let it be heard by those with ears to hear, that the thing inside will do wonders for the man who asks it: Come out and do your worst!'

So Jack took the bag—it was long and thin and heavy—and travelled as far that night as the inn.

'And what wonder do you have with you tonight, Jack?' asked the innkeeper, all smiles.

'Oh, a marvellous thing, but not for strangers to see,' whispered Jack. (He put the bag under his jacket where it would not hear him.) 'If I were to say, "Come out and do your worst"—ah! then you would see a wonder!'

The innkeeper only polished a glass and shrugged.

But after Jack had gone to bed, he and his wife and his brother and his wife's mother all danced a jig on the stairs. 'The lad's a fool and fools don't deserve marvels,' they said, and stole the bag from the foot of Jack's bed.

'Come out and do your worst!' said the innkeeper.

'Come out and do your worst!' said his wife.

'Come out and do your worst,' said his brother.

'Come out and do your worst,' said his wife's mother.

They were not left wanting for wonders. Out of the bag slid an enormous wooden club, and it began to swing and bat, thrash and clout for all it was worth. It chased the innkeeper and his family right out of the inn, over hill and fields, over the horizon, and under the rainbow.

So Jack and his mother left their draughty cottage and moved to the inn, where they found their magic cow munching hay in the barn and their magic tablecloth hidden in a drawer. 'Oh, Jack, Jack, you're a hero and a wonder, and the wife's not born who's good enough to marry you!' said his old mother fondly.

After that, the inn door stood open to any traveller who passed by. In fact the door was never shut—not even to the North Wind when he swooped and whistled out of a bitter sky and set the chimney rattling.

The Old Lady Next Door

If it had not been for Vassia's doll, who knows what might have become of her? Vassia's doll was given her by her mother, and that made her special. But Kookolka was special in other ways, too. How many dolls can eat and talk, for instance? And Kookolka was clever—almost as clever as Vassia's mother when she gave the doll to her daughter, saying: 'Keep her always by you, Vassy. And if ever you are in trouble, ask her advice.'

Soon after that, Vassy was indeed in trouble, deep trouble. Her dear mother died, and her father married again—a fearful, cruel woman with two daughters more cruel and fearful still. Whenever her father was away on business (and that was often) Kasha and Masha and their mother did everything they could to make life unbearable. They ordered Vassy about like a slave, keeping her skivvying from morning till night.

'Oh, Kookolka, doll dear, share this food of mine and tell me what to do!' Vassy would say, breaking off a corner of hard black bread for Kookolka to eat. 'My sisters tell me I must dig the vegetable patch and paint the chicken run and wash the curtains and scour the stove—and all by sunset!'

Then Kookolka would nod and nibble, nibble and nod, and smile at Vassy with her red-thread lips. 'I know a little bed of primroses in the wood. Why don't you go and have a sleep there, my dear, while I consider the problem.' So Vassy went and slept on the primroses, dreaming golden dreams, and when she woke—gracious and goodness!—the chicken coop was painted, the vegetable patch dug, the curtains were drying on the line, and the stove was sparkling. Also Kookolka was back in Vassy's pocket.

Every day Vassy grew more and more beautiful, but not her sisters. They plotted such plots against Vassy and they grew so furious when their plots did not work that their foreheads were soon creased and their mouths permanently puckered. Consequently, the young men in town never looked at Masha or Kasha. They only gazed in wonder at Vassia.

'That does it! The girl must go!' declared their mother. 'And here's the way it shall be done . . .'

Kasha and Masha did as their mother told them and snuffed all the lights in the house—the candles and the lamps. They even poured water into the stove to put out the glowing cinders. Then they shouted, 'Vassia! Lazy girl! Light the lamps! Cook the breakfast! Heat us water for our baths!'

'But there's no light in the house,' said Vassy. 'The stove is cold and all the lamps are out.'

'Oh dear, oh dear, oh dear,' sneered her stepmother. 'Then you'd best go to our neighbour and ask for a flame. Well? What are you waiting for?'

Vassy was waiting for the beat to come back to her heart, for the sickness to go from her stomach, for the terror to drain out of her. 'Go next door? To Baba Yaga?'

Now the only other house for miles around belonged to Baba Yaga, the witch woman. The house itself was terrifying enough, for its garden fence was made of bones, its thatch of human hair, and it ran about on four chicken legs, up and down, to and fro, here and there. In place of bolts were two human hands, and in place of the latch a snarling mouth jagged with teeth. But Baba Yaga was far more fearful than her house, for she flew about in a giant mortar, punting her way through the air with the pestle and sweeping away all trace of her journey with a twig broom. And, of course, she ATE anyone who strayed too close to her house.

'Oh, Kookolka, doll dear, share this food of mine and tell me what to do! My sisters want me to go to the house of Baba Yaga to fetch a light. Give me a flame, won't you, so that I can light the stove again?'

Kookolka nibbled and nodded, nodded and nibbled her share of Vassy's dry black bread. But she would not give Vassy a flame. 'Put me in your pocket and don't be afraid. Who knows? Some good may come of a visit to Baba Yaga.'

Vassy was horrified, but she did as she was told, and with Kookolka in her pocket, she trudged into the dark wood which held Baba

Yaga's dreadful cottage. As she walked, a horseman overtook her—a horseman dressed in white on a white horse with white bridle and saddle, as darting as light. About noon, another horseman overtook her—a horseman all in red, on a red horse with red bridle and saddle, as hot as fire. All day it took her to walk to Baba Yaga's house, and just as she reached the bony fence, a third horseman shot by her, stirring up the leaves in clouds. He was all in black, on a black horse with a black bridle and saddle—and he appeared to ride straight through the wall of the cottage and disappear from sight!

Behind him came Baba Yaga!

'Oho! Oho! Supper on legs!' croaked the old witch in a voice like a roosting rook. 'What brings you here, girly?' Her mortar swooped so low over Vassy's head that it stood her hair on end.

'My stepmother sent me to ask for a light,' whispered Vassy, clutching the doll in her pocket, her eyes tight shut in terror.

But Baba Yaga did not club her with the giant pestle or tear her with her long nails. 'Very well. But I don't do favours. If you want a light, you must work for it. If your work is satisfactory, you shall have your flame. If not, I shall have you—and a tender little mouthful you'll make, for sure. Open, house!'

The house crabbed a few steps to the right, a few to the left on its chicken legs, then the bolt-hands unclasped and the latch-mouth closed, and the door

opened to Baba Yaga. 'Fetch me some dinner!' commanded Baba Yaga, and Vassy ran here and there, finding whatever she could. Everything she brought—salad, apples, cold meat, raw meat, porridge, and bread—Baba Yaga wolfed down, until the cupboards were bare. Then she ate the shelves from the cupboards and the coal from the fire, before wiping her mouth on her sleeve. 'Tomorrow you can clean all the wheat in that cornbin—sort grains from husks,' she told Vassy. 'And see it's done before I get home, or I'll EAT you. Hands! Hands! Come!'

Suddenly three pairs of hands—no bodies, no arms, just hands—appeared out of thin air, cleared the table, plumped the pillow on Baba Yaga's bed, and laid her gently down there. One pair of hands was white, one pair red, and one pair black. Then with a clap—one clap, two clap, three clap—all three disappeared.

Next morning, away went Baba Yaga punting her pestle, and Vassy opened the cornbin. It stood as high as the ceiling and was full to the brim with wheat and husks, all mixed up together.

'Oh, Kookolka, doll dear, share these crumbs with me and tell me what to do! It will take a lifetime to clean this wheat!!'

Kookolka climbed out of her apron pocket and took the few crumbs from Vassy's palm. 'I saw a clump of bluebells in the garden. Go and pick some for the old woman—and don't worry.' So Vassy went and picked bluebells, and put them in vases all about the house. While she was outside, those horsemen rode up again—in at the gate and right through the house—first white, then red, then black. Vassy remembered the three pairs of hands. The third was no sooner past than dusk fell and Baba Yaga came speeding home, her mortar spinning, her pestle pushing, her broom sweeping away all trace of her passage through the forest. 'Open, door!' she screeched as she came.

Baba Yaga looked around her at the bluebells. 'And is it done? The work? Or am I to eat you for supper?' Heaving the lid off the cornbin she squinnied inside, and there—gracious and goodness!—were a dozen bushels of clean wheat. 'Oho, do I smell magic?' said the witch woman in a voice like a crooked crow. 'How came the impossible done by a young girl like you?'

'Please, ma'am, by reason that my mother loved me, I suppose,' said Vassy, curtsying. 'I'll just fetch your dinner.'

Once again the witch woman ate as much as an army of men, and again the three pairs of hands—white, red, and black—cleared the table and carried her to bed.

'Tomorrow your job is to part the poppy seeds from the gravel!' croaked a sleepy voice out of the darkness. 'Or I'll EAT you!'

On the second day, Vassy's doll sorted the million poppy seeds in the seedbin from a million grains of grey gravel, while Vassy cooked a delicious vegetable stew for the old witch. Again the horsemen thundered through the gate, through the garden, through the house—white, red, and

black. Again, dark fell and the witch was home again—push-swish, push-swish. 'Oho! Oho! I smell magic here!' she said, running the poppy seeds through her bony fingers. 'How came the impossible done by a young girl like you?'

'Please, ma'am, by reason that my mother loved me, I suppose,' said Vassy curtsying. 'I cooked you a special stew for dinner.'

Baba Yaga began to warm towards the young girl. 'Say, child, is there anything that puzzles you about this strange world?'

'There is,' said Vassy. 'Who are the horsemen I saw out there, in the forest—one white, one red, one black?'

'Oho! One is my bright dawn, one my red noon, one my dark knight!' said Baba Yaga and peered keenly into Vassy's pretty face. 'What else?'

'When I am older, I shall be wiser,' said Vassia politely. 'It would be rude to pester you with any more questions.'

'Oho! Oho! Well said!' cried the witch woman, leaping up and down with delight and shaking both her bony arms. 'If you had asked me one question about the inside of my house, I would have had to EAT you. As it is, you may have your light and go. But don't forget your old granny Yaga when your life changes for the better.'

She gave Vassia a tiny candle in a little candlestick, and sent her out into the night. Oddly enough, the light from the candle, small as it was, lit the forest path quite clearly. And though wolves howled, and owls hooted, after three days in the house of Baba Yaga, Vassia was not afraid of anything.

'Oh. It's you,' said Kasha, heartbroken to see her pretty stepsister safe home again.

'What took you so long?' said Masha, snatching the candle. 'You've been gone four days and here's us with no warmth, no light, and no hot water to wash in!'

But before Vassia could tell them everything that had happened, the flame of the little candle jumped off its wick and began to flit about the room. It grew bigger, too, until like a ball of lightning, it was rolling around the walls of the house, setting light to the curtains, the rugs, the bedding. Kasha, Masha, and their mother screamed and ran out of the house in their night clothes. Away they went through the forest, the flame splitting into three to chase them, three roaring fireballs which lit

their flying plaits like the wicks of candles and drowned out their noise with incendiary crackling.

Vassia stood in the garden and watched her home burn down, enjoying the rosy silence, the scent of woodsmoke, savouring her freedom. She picked out of the ashes her few belongings (Kookolka was safe in her pocket, of course) and walked back through the forest to Baba Yaga's house, to tell her the news.

But instead of the chicken-legged house, she found only a little cottage, and living there a frail old lady with no one in the world to look after her.

'May I lodge with you, Grandma?' said Vassia politely. 'If you buy flax, I can spin and weave it, and you can sell the cloth and keep the money. Like that, we may get by until my father comes home.'

The lady was very glad of Vassia's company and of her sensible suggestion. She went out at once and, with her last copeck, bought all the flax she could afford.

'Oh, Kookolka, doll dear,' said Vassy when she had the flax in her lap. 'Share this last crust of mine and then please help me spin my flax.'

Kookolka nodded and nibbled, nibbled and nodded. And of course Kookolka spun the flax far finer than any human hands could do, so that when it was woven into cloth, there was no softer, finer-woven piece of linen from Moscow to Petrograd.

'I'll take it to the Tsar!' cried the old lady. 'No one else in all Russia is good enough to wear such cloth on his back!' So the linen was presented to the Tsar, and he rewarded the gift with gifts of his own, saying, 'I have never seen cloth like it!'

But—goodness and gracious!—the weave was so very fine that the Tsar's tailor had no needle sharp enough to sew it into a shirt! And though tailors were sent for from Kiev and Omsk and Archangel, none of them could sew the linen either.

So the Tsar sent for the old woman and said, 'Grandma, I'm afraid you will have to sew this for me. You have made it so fine that my tailor cannot pass a needle through it!'

'Bless you, Majesty, I didn't make it,' said the old woman. 'A young woman staying in my house spun it and wove it. And she is more beautiful than the cloth itself.'

'Then you'd better send her to me,' said the Tsar.

Vassia was sent for, and took back the linen, and asked dolly Kookolka to sew it into a shirt for the Tsar. Now whether Kookolka sewed magic into the seams, or whether the old woman was less ordinary than she

seemed, or whether Vassy was more beautiful than I told you—when she placed the shirt in the Tsar's lap, he asked her to marry him, then and there—said he would have no other bride out of all Russia. And Vassia agreed.

Her father came home from business to a surprise or two—his house burned down, his wife and stepdaughters gone, his little Vassy betrothed to the Tsar. But he ran all the way to the palace and was there in time to see the ceremony. Vassia looked more beautiful than ever. And though many at the wedding wondered: 'Goodness and gracious! A wedding dress with pockets?'—Vassia said the pocket was for her doll and that she would go nowhere without Kookolka—not even to the altar.

Snow White

There was once a king who loved his daughter more than his kingdom, thought her black hair softer than night, her red lips more precious than rubies, her snow white skin lovelier than silk. But the child's mother was dead, and the king married again—a handsome woman named Grimalda—thinking his new wife could not fail to love Princess Snow White.

The new queen had a magic mirror, and every time the moon was full, she would ask the moonlit glass:

> 'Mirror, mirror in my hand,
> Who is the fairest in the land?'
> And the mirror would answer:
> 'I cannot speak but what is true:
> No one is fairer, queen, than you.'

But though the queen's face was beautiful, her nature was not. She envied Snow White her place in the king's heart, looked on her black hair, red lips, and white skin as fondly as coal and blood and sleet, and wished her away. Besides, she could not fail to see how every day Snow White grew more and more beautiful.

One day, when the moon was full, the wicked queen asked her moonlit magic glass,

> '*Mirror, mirror in my hand,*
> *Who is the fairest in the land?*'
> And the mirror answered:
> '*I cannot speak but what is true:*
> *Snow White is fairer, queen, than you.*'

In her jealousy, the queen spat at the moon. 'Then she must die!' she cried, and the moon turned a little paler hearing it.

Summoning the royal huntsman, the wicked Grimalda said, 'Take Snow White into the forest, beyond paths, beyond tracks. And when you reach the darkest place . . . kill her. Bring me her heart, so that I may be certain you have obeyed me!'

The huntsman dared not refuse. But as he walked into the trackless forest, Snow White's little hand in his, he was glad of the shadows to hide his tears. At the centre of the forest, he pulled out his long-bladed knife with one hand while with the other he cupped Snow White's face. He saw her hair, black as the raven, saw her lips, red as the wild rose, saw her skin, whiter than the moon with fright. 'I can't do it, child. I can't kill you. The soul inside me forbids it. Run, child! Run and hide! Run, and don't stop running till you are out of this benighted land and into a better one. Run!'

Slipping and skidding on fallen leaves, Snow White fled. No hunted fawn, no songbird chased with nets ever fled as blindly as the panic-stricken princess. Through brambles and thickets, clearings and ditches, she ran on and on, the breath sobbing in her throat. The moonlight fell on her between the leaves like cold drops of water, and the mud plastered her skirts to her legs; her shoes filled up with stones.

Meanwhile, the huntsman killed a boar, cut out its heart, and took the heart to the queen, on a silver dish, to prove Snow White was dead. The queen believed him and laughed a strange, hooting laugh like a bittern booming on fog-bound marshes. The king believed it, too—believed his daughter had been killed by wild beasts in the forest. But though he searched and searched, he found no rag, no bone, no hank of black hair. It was as though Snow White had melted away.

All night Snow White wandered the deep, dark forests, lost and in despair. In the morning, she found a cottage—a wee building hardly bigger than a chicken shed and almost as ramshackle.

She called out, but no one answered. She knocked at the door, but nobody came. She ducked inside, and found seven little chairs round a table strewn with seven dirty bowls, knives, forks, and spoons. And she wondered, 'Are there other children like me in this forest?'

Upstairs, there were seven little beds, side by side. Chilled and exhausted, Snow White said to herself, 'Yesterday I was almost killed and if I die tomorrow, at least I have lived one more day.' And she lay down across all seven little beds and went to sleep.

When she woke, she thought she must have fallen into Fairyland, for seven small men were looking at her over the footrail of the bed. 'Is this your house?' she whispered.

'Just like it, and just where we left it this morning. But of course we could be mistaken, for there was no girl on our beds this morning.' Their ears were leafy and their hair like the tufts of sheep's wool that snag on briars.

When Snow White told them her name and her story, their eyes grew large as plums and filled with tears. 'You must stay with us, princess,' they said, 'and we shall love you as you should rightly have been loved all along. Only care for us a little, if you can.'

So Snow White stayed on in the little cottage, and cooked and sewed for the seven woodsmen. She mended their roof, too, when it leaked. And their boots. Before the moon had waned and waxed once more, she had grown very fond of her seven friends.

Each morning, as they set off to work, they warned her, 'Lock the door and don't open—no, not to knocking or calling. One day the queen may find out you are here, and if she does, she won't come with kisses in her pocket.'

They were right. One night, when the moon was full, the wicked Queen Grimalda asked of her magic glass:

'*Mirror, mirror in my hand,*
Who is the fairest in the land?'
and the mirror replied:
'*I cannot speak but what is true.*
Snow White is fairer far than you.'

At that, the queen spat at the stars. 'Not dead? Then where is she? Tell me! I must know!' And, because it had no power to lie, the mirror told the queen the way to the cottage in the woods.

First the blackbirds stopped singing. Then there came a knock on the door. 'Greetings to the lady of the house! Won't you open to an old tinker woman and see my tray of pretty things?'

Snow White remembered the words of the seven woodsmen, and peeped cautiously out of the window, to see if it was the queen. But it was only a ragged gypsy, peddling ribbons and buttons and belts. So she opened the door and gazed in delight at all the colourful things on the tray. Prettiest of all was a belt plaited from white leather. 'How much is the belt?' she asked.

'Because your skin is just as white and soft, you may have it for nothing,' said the gypsy. 'Let me put it on for you.' And she put the belt round Snow White's waist and pulled it tight.

Tight and tighter she pulled it, sharp and cruel and fierce. 'Oh! I can't breathe!' cried Snow White, but the gypsy only pulled harder and harder, until the princess fainted for want of air and fell to the ground.

Then the wicked Queen Grimalda threw off her ragged disguise. 'Dead at last!' she crowed and swaggered back to the palace.

When the seven woodsmen came home, they found Snow White lying across the threshold as white as death. At once they cut the leather of the belt, and with a cry like a woodcock, she drew in a great breath. And when she saw the seven anxious faces looking at her, she laughed and said, 'I may die tomorrow, but at least I have lived another day!'

'Mirror, mirror, in my hand,
Who is the fairest in the land?'
asked the wicked queen
when next the moon was full.
'I cannot speak but what is true;
Snow White is fairer far than you,'
replied the mirror.

In her fury, the queen spat at the sky. 'Not dead? Then I must try harder!' she cried, and wanting a better disguise than before, conjured herself the face and body of an old lady.

First the thrushes stopped singing, and then there came a knock at the door and a voice at the keyhole. 'Pretty trinkets! Lovely things for a lovely girl! Open and see!'

Snow White remembered the words of the seven woodsmen, and peeped down from an upstairs window. But when she saw the grey hair, the stooping back, the weather-beaten ugly face, she knew it could not be the queen and opened the door. 'How much is that pretty comb?' she asked.

'Because it shines like your glossy black hair, dearie, you may have it for nothing. Let me comb out the tangles.' And she began to comb Snow White's jet black hair.

But with every stroke of the comb, the princess felt the strength drain from her arms, from her legs, from her heart—'Stop, please!'—until with a sigh she crumpled to the ground. The wicked Grimalda laughed aloud and snarled the comb deep into Snow White's hair. 'Dead at last!' she crowed and, throwing off her magic disguise, straightened her

willowy back. Still, some of the magic clung to
her, and she walked back to the palace more
slowly this time, aching, as if a grain of old age had
lodged in her bones.

When the seven woodsmen came home, they
found Snow White sprawled across the threshold,
white as death, though with no sign of a hurt.
They searched for many minutes before they
found the comb tangled in her hair and pulled it
free. With a cry like a gull, she opened her eyes
and drew in a great breath. Then seeing the seven
anxious faces leaning over her she smiled and said,
'I may die tomorrow, but at least I have lived one
more day!'

'Mirror, mirror in my hand
Now who's fairest in the land?'
asked the wicked queen when
next the moon was full.
'I cannot speak but what is true;
Snow White is fairer far than you,'
replied the moonlit mirror.

In her rage, the queen spat at the mirror, but
only succeeded in dirtying her own reflection. She
saw her mouth twist as it formed the words: 'Next
time I shall not fail!'

First the larks stopped singing. Then there came

a knock at the door and a voice at the keyhole and a rattling of the lock. 'Fine juicy apples! Buy my fine juicy apples!'

'No,' said Snow White through the locked door. 'I never open the door to strangers.'

'Quite right, quite right,' said the deep, dark voice outside. 'Won't you open the window and just see my apples?'

Snow White remembered the gypsy and the old woman and the words of the seven woodsmen. But when she looked out of the window and saw a handsome young man with a basket of rosy apples, she could see no harm in the world. 'How much is one apple?'

'Because your lips are as red as any apple, take one and welcome.'

So Snow White reached down and took an apple . . . then she put it back. No, no. It may be poisoned, she thought.

'Do you fear it's sour, lassie? Do you fear it's wormy?' chuckled the young man, and took a great cracking, juicy bite from the green of the apple. 'See? Quite safe to eat.'

So Snow White laughed with relief and took the apple from the young man's hand and bit into it—bit into the rosy red side . . . bit into the side painted with scarlet poison.

With a cry like a swan shot from the sky, Snow White fell to the floor. 'Dead at last!' cried the wicked queen, shrugging off her magic disguise. Rushing home to the magic mirror, she at once pulled it out and began to ask:

'Mirror mirror in my hand . . .'

But the reflection in the mirror was so ugly, so lined by hatred and cruelty and jealousy, that Grimalda could not bear to look at it and thrust the mirror away, deep under her pillows.

When the seven woodsmen came home, they found Snow White lying on the floor of the cottage. Though they searched her hair, her hands, her pockets, they could find no reason for her death, but could only cry and keen and sorrow at the loss of their dear, dear princess.

They could not bear to bury her in the dank, wormy ground, so they made a glass coffin, and placed her inside it, in the full face of the sun. At first they could only sit and gaze at her pale, lifeless loveliness. But after a time there was work to be done, and they would visit her each evening with flowers and fresh tears.

So Snow White's body in her glass coffin was quite alone the day the prince rode by. Lost in the forest he stopped at the cottage to ask the way. Seeing the coffin in the garden, he stopped to look at the young girl inside. Stopping to look, he found he could not look away, for she was the loveliest girl he had ever seen. He was still there, gazing and gazing, when the seven woodsmen came home that evening.

'Her name was Snow White,' said the oldest, startling the prince who had not heard them coming. 'A princess and as sweet-natured as she was beautiful.'

When the prince heard her story, he was filled with such a passion of grief that he struck the coffin with his fist, and cracked it clean across. When he saw the breeze ruffle Snow White's clothes and stir her raven-black

hair, he struck his chest as though to break the heart inside. Then he gathered Snow White up in his arms and kissed her full on the mouth.

The piece of poisoned apple lodged in her throat was shaken loose, and Snow White woke up with a cry of happiness. When she saw the prince's face close up to her own, she smiled and said, 'I may die tomorrow, but at least I have known what it is to be in love.'

The queen dreamt that the moon rose blood red and that the stars were falling on her. She thrust her hand under the pillow and pulled out her magic looking-glass.

 *'Mirror, mirror in my hand*
Who is the fairest in the land?'
And the mirror answered:
'Lovely Snow White, happy bride
Is the fairest far and wide,
But fairer still will be her heir—
The little daughter she will bear.'

The queen's rage knew no bounds, no depths, no end. She smashed the mirror against the moonlit wall—and in that very instant, fell dead.

But her soul? Oh, her soul was in that mirror—had been for many years. And that lived on, trapped for ever within a thousand broken shards of glass, and a magic circle of ebony.

Meanwhile, Snow White dreamed that the moon leaned down from the sky to kiss her. But when she woke, she found it was only the prince, her husband. So she smiled, kissed him back, turned over and went back to sleep.

The Three Oranges

There was once a king who wanted, and did not want, his daughter to marry. So anxious was he to take care of her that he would have kept her in a box if he could and taken her out only to dust. Instead, he built a crystal mountain—a pyramid of steeply sloping glass, a transparent icicle one hundred feet high. And there at the top he placed a throne, where Princess Purity could sit and watch the world without any danger of it harming her.

'If any man can climb to the top of the glass mountain,' he decreed, 'and take the three oranges lying in my daughter's lap, he may marry her, and I shall give him half my kingdom!'

Each morning and evening, the rising or the setting sun shone through the glass mountain making rainbow flickers. But Princess Purity was lovelier even than the flickering rainbows. And so suitors came from all over the world to try for the three oranges she held in her lap.

They went up barefoot and in boots. They rode up on horseback and in chariots. They brought axes to cut hand-holds, and ladders to climb. But their feet and boots slipped, their axes broke, their ladders toppled

and their horses and chariots tumbled off the glassy cliff on top of them. No one got so much as head-high off the ground.

The crowds who gathered at the bottom of the mountain clouded the glass with their breath. But Princess Purity had to go on sitting, in lonely splendour, like an angel on a spire of ice.

* * *

'Another night like this and we shan't have any hay to sell,' said Farmer Herbert to his three sons.

They stood in Home Meadow and looked around them. All the tall, lush, green grass which had waved in yesterday's wind was cut as short as a shaver's beard.

'What did it, Dad?' asked Bigg Herbert, the oldest son.

'That's for you to find out,' said his father. 'Keep watch in Near Meadow tonight and make sure the thief doesn't come back for more. . . . And mind you don't fall asleep!'

So Bigg Herbert spent that night in Near Meadow, under the apple tree there. And he did not fall asleep—or so he said. 'No, I saw the moon rise, and the stars come out. I felt the wind get up and the tree sway. But then the ground began to rumble and the earth began to shake . . . so I ran for my life!'

Next morning, Near Meadow was cut as short as a monk's hair. 'Another raid like this and we shan't have enough hay to last the winter,' said Farmer Herbert.

'Who did it, Dad?' asked Lessor Herbert, the second son.

'That's for you to find out,' said his father. 'Keep watch in Middle Meadow tonight, and make sure the thief doesn't come back for more. And mind you don't fall asleep like your worthless brother. Earthquakes and rumblings, indeed!'

So Lessor Herbert spent that night in Middle Meadow, under the chestnut tree. And he did not fall asleep—or so he said. 'I saw the moon rise and the stars come out. I felt the wind get up and the tree sway. But then the ground began to rumble and the earth began to shake . . . so I ran for my life, or it would have got me, it would, whatever it was!'

Next morning, Middle Meadow was cut as short as the hair on an egg. 'Another disaster like this and we shall be ruined,' said Farmer Herbert. 'Earthquakes and rumblings, bah!'

'I'll keep watch tonight,' said Scruffy Herbert, the farmer's third son. Scruffy's job on the farm was mucking out, so he was always smelly and filthy. His father and brothers had quite forgotten what he looked like underneath all the muck and grime.

'You?!' sneered his brothers. 'You're no use in the daytime, let alone at night!'

But Farmer Herbert did let Scruffy Herbert keep watch in Far Meadow, sitting under the oak tree there. And he did not fall asleep.

No. He saw the moon rise, the stars come out. He felt the wind get up and the tree sway. He felt the ground tremble and the earth quake, and he saw the great white horse whose hooves were making all the din.

It leapt the fence and began to eat the grass in Far Meadow.

Scruffy Herbert did not run away. He climbed up the oak tree and, when the horse came to graze beneath the tree, dropped down on to its back, knotting his fingers in the mane. At once the horse raised its head and cantered away, carrying Scruffy over field and hill—as gentle and obedient as if Scruffy had always been its master.

In the morning, Scruffy went home on foot. 'You shan't be troubled any more, Dad,' he said.

His brothers jeered and sneered. 'Why? Did you scare off the evil magic with your ugly face?' Scruffy said nothing. He took no notice. He did not mention the little matter of the horse.

With only one field to reap and bale and stack, the Herbert boys finished harvesting early that year. 'So can Lessor and me go to see the Glass Mountain?' said Bigg. 'Everyone's going. They say the princess is real beautiful and princes are coming from all over to try the climb.' Farmer Herbert said they could go.

'Can I come?' said Scruffy, but they only threw a bale of hay at him: 'If the princess caught a whiff of you, she might fall off her mountain! Go and spread muck.'

Bigg and Lessor joined the crowds around the base of the glass mountain, and gazed and gawped at all the princes in their armour, the pedlars selling things, the jugglers performing, and, of course, the suitors sliding helplessly down the glassy slopes on their faces, horses, bottoms, and chariots. It was quite a circus.

Suddenly, cantering through the crowd came a young man on a huge and beautiful white horse. He was dressed in green velvet, with felt boots and a belt of red copper, and he set his horse right at the mountain. It fairly leapt up the glass precipice. Halfway to the top, though, the horse stopped.

Princess Purity, who had sunk into a kind of sleepy misery on her mountaintop throne, stared in amazement. The most handsome face she had ever seen was looking up at her. So much did she like the face that she threw one of her oranges to the young man, who caught it, before his sure-footed horse slithered back down the glass slope on its hocks.

'You should have seen it!' said Bigg and Lessor at home that night.

'I wish I had,' said Scruffy.

But his brothers threw rotten sprout-tops at him and jeered, 'Sorry: no dogs allowed in the palace grounds.'

Next day Bigg and Lessor went back. There were no princes left among the watching crowd: they had all tried and failed to win the princess. Bigg stood on Lessor's shoulders. But as soon as he set one foot on the glass, he slithered down again, squashing his brother.

Suddenly, through the crowd came a young man on a huge and beautiful white horse. He was dressed in blue velvet, with felt boots and a belt of silver links, and he set his horse right at the mountain. It fairly leapt up the glass precipice.

Princess Purity, who was still thinking about the face she had seen the day before, heard the clatter of hooves on glass and looked down to see the same face. Higher and higher it came. A reaching hand brushed the tips of her shoes. She slipped an orange into the hand. Then horse and rider slithered back down the glass mountain, though the horse kept its feet and galloped away uninjured.

'You should have seen it!' said Bigg and Lessor at home that night.

'I wish I had,' said Scruffy.

But his brothers only threw rotten mangelwurzels at him, and said, 'Sorry, no pigs allowed in the palace grounds.'

Next day, Bigg and Lessor went back to the glass
mountain. Lessor stood on Bigg's shoulders. But
though he jumped as high as he could, he only slid
down, like a monkey on a greased pole, and squashed
his brother flat.

Suddenly, through the crowd came a young man on a huge and
beautiful white horse. He was dressed in scarlet velvet, with felt boots
and a belt of gold coins, and he set his horse right at the mountain. It
fairly leapt up the glass precipice.

It was him again! Princess Purity stood up to urge him on. Her
fingers dug deep into the third orange, and juice ran down her silken
skirts. Up and up the sure-footed horse ran—Purity could feel the
clatter of its hooves on the glass, see its nostrils flaring, feel the heat
from its flanks. The young man loomed up over the peak of the glass
mountain. She held out to him the last orange, but he swept up both
her and her orange in his arms and, in one bound, launched his horse
off the mountain and down to the ground. Pausing only to set the
princess down at the palace gate, the young man in red velvet galloped
away into the evening gloom.

The king came running out, the crowd milled about, the mountain
crazed, cracked, and tinkled into a thousand fragments.

'Oh, you should have seen it!' exclaimed Bigg and Lessor
that night.

'I wish I had,' said Scruffy.

But his brothers threw handfuls of broken glass at
him and said, 'Fine guest you would make at a
royal wedding, dung beetle!'

Even so, the whole family went to the

palace park next day. Everyone in the world seemed to be there. For the king had called on the Chevalier of the Three Oranges to present himself and claim his bride.

'Come forward, whatever prince has achieved those three oranges and the love of my daughter!' cried the king. But no prince came forward (though there were dozens there) because no prince had the three oranges.

'Well then, come forward whatever knight has achieved those three oranges and the love of my daughter!' cried the king. But no knight came forward either (though there were hundreds there) because no knight had the three oranges.

'Well, somebody must have it!' said the king, rather desperately. 'Come forward whoever you are, or my daughter will never forgive me!'

Scruffy edged forward through the crowd.

'Where do you think you're going?' said his brothers.

'I just want to see the princess,' said Scruffy.

Then all at once he was at the front of the crowd and walking towards the king, and kneeling down on one knee.

'What's the fool up to?' said Farmer Herbert.

The king held his nose, then forgot to hold it. For out of the pockets of Scruffy's stinking clothes came first one, then two, then three oranges, the third rather squished and spoiled. Then Scruffy threw off his work clothes, and underneath he was wearing . . . red velvet. But not until he had washed his hands and face in the

fountain did he shake the king's hand and kiss Princess Purity, to the cheers of the crowd.

When he whistled softly, his magic horse (who had eaten up three meadows and run three times up the glass mountain) came cantering through the crowds, bowling over Bigg and Lessor as it came. Lifting Purity into the saddle, Scruffy mounted behind her, and together they rode to the cathedral to be married.

Shocking to say, the king ate oranges all through the ceremony, and got sticky right up to his elbows.

The Thirteenth Child

When the queen had a baby boy, the king was delighted and gave him a silver spoon on a cord to wear round his neck. The queen, too, was happy, thinking the next child might be a girl. When the second was a boy, he too was lovely. He too was given a spoon. But the queen did hope her next child would be a girl. Or the next. Or the next. At last, king and queen were blessed with twelve sons—big-boned, bonny boys, bold as bears, each wearing his spoon like a battle medal. The king was hugely happy, but the queen's wish had become a desperate longing.

One winter's day, when the princes were particularly noisy and rough playing snowballs, the queen went, for peace and quiet, to prune her rose garden. A thorn pricked her finger, and blood fell on to the snowy ground.

'If only I had a daughter with skin as white as snow and lips as red as blood,' said the queen to herself. A snowball hit her on the back. 'If I had a daughter like that, those boys could fly away, for all I care.'

It was a terrible thing to say—not meant, hardly meant. But the words hung in the air as a frosty smoke, while her blood dripped on to the snow. Soon the queen was expecting another child—the thirteenth. And the thirteenth was a daughter.

The baby's first cry pierced the air like a thorn, and in the same instant, all the windows of the palace blew open. At first, the twelve princes thought they had been smothered by an avalanche of snow. Then each looked down and found himself . . . transformed: in place of boots, webbed feet, in place of a face, a beak, in place of arms a pair of wings, in place of skin, feathers. All twelve had turned into wild ducks. Through the open window of the palace they flew away—a chevron in the sky, an arrowhead of migrating ducks.

The queen finally had her daughter, and the daughter was as lovely as any rose garden, with blood-red lips and snow-white skin. She too was given her silver spoon. Princess Snow-Rose was a dear, loving child. And yet never a day passed but she felt some dark and terrible sadness haunting the palace, which no one would talk about. She was lonely, too.

'If only I had brothers and sisters to play with,' she began to say one day—and her mother promptly burst into tears! The whole terrible story came out—how her twelve brothers had been turned into wild ducks and had flown away.

'And all because of me,' she whispered, chilling outside and in. 'I wish that I had never been born. I must go and find them, and save them, even if it costs me my life.'

Nothing the king or queen said could change her mind. She took no purse and she took no carriage, but walked through the world till she was ragged. For three years she walked.

One woodland morning, a skein of twelve ducks flurried up into the sky ahead of her. At just the spot where they had taken off, she found a little cottage, and in the cottage twelve chairs round a table, and on the table twelve silver spoons.

I have found them! she thought, dizzy with excitement and hunger. Now all I have to do is wait for them to come home. Porridge was cooking on the stove. She ate a bowlful, using her own silver spoon, then lay down on one of the twelve beds and fell asleep.

With a rattle of wings, the twelve brothers flew home at nightfall. As the last ray of sunlight left the sky, their feathers dropped down in a snowy moult, and they were themselves again—twelve handsome young men (who looked a lot like the king). Sitting down to supper, they picked up their spoons to eat. And there, glittering on the table, lay a thirteenth spoon!

The oldest boy knocked over his chair with a clatter. 'Up and search, brothers! Who can this spoon belong to but our sister—our curse and our sorrow—the cause of all our misery!'

They tore open the cupboards, they overturned the table. They slashed at the curtains and ripped the covers from the beds. But as, at the twelfth bed, brothers and sister came face to face for the first time, and daggers were drawn, the youngest prince raised his voice.

'Stop! Don't kill her! How can she be to blame for what happened to us? She was not three seconds old when the enchantment fell on us.'

Snow-Rose stood up on the bed, her face streaming with tears, her shadow dancing in the lamplight. 'For three years I have searched for you. If killing me will free you from this enchantment, please— kill me now. Otherwise, tell me how to lift the spell and I will do it!'

'Impossible,' said the oldest brother.

'You couldn't,' said another.

'We shall always be ducks by day and men by night.'

'No remedy.'

'What? Weave shirts from nettles?'

'Weave twelve shirts from nettles?'

'And not weep?'

'And not speak, all that while?'

'Impossible.'

'No. We shall always be as we are,' said the youngest prince.

Snow-Rose said nothing in reply, only nodded her head, unsmiling, dry-eyed. Tomorrow she would begin work. Twelve shirts for twelve ducks. And not a word or a tear or a laugh till the last shirt was made.

Each morning she left the cottage at the same time as her brothers flew off into the cornfields to feed. But Snow-Rose waded, instead, waist-deep into the nettle patch, and gathered up swaithes of nettles in her arms.

Like a million hot pinpricks they stung the tender white creases of her arms, her hands, her throat, her face. But she shed not a tear. Carding, spinning, weaving the nettles into cloth, her poor hands throbbed, livid and red, but she never once cried out in pain.

Watching her, the princes soon saw just how much she loved them, and loved her in return. They begged her but she spoke not one word in reply.

For then it would all be for nothing.

Weeks turned to months, months to a year. The nettles were all gone from round the cottage— gone throughout the wood. And Snow-Rose had to fetch nettles home miles, in bales on her back. And she worked all day and half the night. Soon all that remained was to sew the woven pieces together.

By noon there were only four more shirts to sew. By nightfall the princes would have their shirts, and her ordeal and theirs would be over . . .

Suddenly hoofbeats clamoured through the forest, riders with plumed hats and quivers of yellow arrows.

Arrows!

Snow-Rose thought of her brothers winging home over the treetops. She imagined the hunter's arrows piercing them one by one.

Sweeping together her sewing, swinging the bundle over her shoulder, she pelted after the hunters. She could not call out to them, could not shout a warning to her brothers! In the distance, she could hear the whirr of wings, the creaking cry of her brothers singing out to her for their supper . . .

As the lead huntsman raised his bow, a ragged girl rushed out of the trees and grabbed his bridle, almost unseating him. His arrow flew wide. The ducks flew by overhead, unhurt.

The king whose aim she had spoiled was only angry for a moment; he had rarely seen such a pretty girl as the one now standing in front of his horse. He smiled and asked who she was.

Snow-Rose did not answer.

'Don't be shy. Why did you stop me shooting?' he asked.

But Snow-Rose did not answer, could not answer.

'Come back to the castle with me, won't you, and tell me all about yourself?'

And Snow-Rose had to go—could not tell him how vital it was to get home, to take the shirts home.

* * *

This dumb, ragged, unsmiling beauty intrigued the king, and he soon found himself falling in love with her. It was annoying that she never laughed at his jokes, but something noble and sorrowful spoke to him out of her eyes, so that he was content to sit in silence with her for hours.

But the king's love for Snow-Rose made the ladies of the royal court seethe with jealousy. 'Look at her—all spotty red!' they sneered. 'She probably has some disgusting disease!'

'She never cries when I pinch her at table.'

'Never cries out when I kick her under the table.'

'She's probably a witch. Witches never cry.'

Snow-Rose could not defend herself. When they began to make up lies about her, blame her for everything bad, accuse her of witchcraft and sorcery, Snow-Rose could say nothing in her defence. At last, blood was found on the snow beneath her window, and she was accused of murder. At that, the king's love turned to horror, and he condemned Snow-Rose to death.

'See! See! She doesn't even cry!' jeered the ladies of the court. 'We told you she was a witch!'

As Snow-Rose was led away to a prison cell to await her death at dawn, she made signs that she wanted her bundle of sewing. The prison warder brought it—ooching and ouching—flung it in after her and went away sucking his stinging fingers.

All night Snow-Rose sewed, while outside a bonfire was built of branches and benches and brooms. At the heart of the bonfire was a stake of wood, and round the stake a golden chain. Anyone else would have wept for sheer fear, but Snow-Rose only sewed and stitched, stitched and sewed. Panic swept over her when, at the last moment, she found one sleeve missing: it must have dropped from the bundle as she ran through the woods! Perhaps the magic would fail, for want of that one sleeve. But there was no time to replace it. Morning spilled in at the barred window. The warder's key rattled in the lock.

'Time to die, miss,' he said.

As Snow-Rose walked to the bonfire, she dropped behind her, one by one, twelve coarse and rather odd-smelling green shirts. No sooner did they touch the ground, than wild ducks settled out of the sky, picked them up in their beaks, and flew off with them.

'One last time, I beg you, girl,' said the king. 'Speak and defend yourself against this terrible charge!' But Snow-Rose would not speak, could not speak. So they tied her to the stake and lit the fire around her.

Suddenly hoofbeats clamoured over the castle drawbridge, and into the yard rode twelve princes leaning forward in their saddles, shouting themselves hoarse. They came on at the charge, forcing courtiers and ladies to jump aside. 'Let our sister go, or die on our swords!' they yelled. 'She is innocent of any crime but love!'

The fire was doused, the golden chain snapped, and Snow-Rose leapt down from the bonfire to hug all her twelve brothers. 'You're safe! You're saved!' she cried, and her tears of joy intermingled with sobs of laughter.

Now everything could be explained to the king, and the ladies of the court were put to shame for their lying. The blood on the snow, they admitted, had been nothing more than the blood of a pet duck.

With a shudder, the youngest prince held his cloak tight around him and said to Snow-Rose, 'Let's leave this place and go home.'

'Yes, but I may return here. I have grown rather fond of the king,' said Snow-Rose, 'and I may well marry him . . . But tell me! Did you find the lost sleeve, or was my work enough to recover you all completely?'

'Not completely,' said the youngest brother, and his cloak fell open. In place of his left arm was a duck's wing.

Still, I never heard that he was loved any the less for his strange appearance. Nor, when they returned home to their mother, did she prize her boys any less than her girl—no, not by the breadth of a rose stem, not by the weight of one snowflake.

Tamlin

One day and one week and one year, in the parish of Melrose, Young Tamlin fell from his horse while riding. He fell into the Land of Fairies, and into the power of the Fairy Queen, who dressed him in green velvet and silks but locked up his soul in Fairyland.

When he did not come home, Tamlin's sweetheart Janet wept for him. And after that, she searched for him, asked after him from Melrose to Selkirk. But no one had seen so much as one red hair of Tamlin.

All they had seen was a highwayman dressed in green, a robber with red hair, who stopped maidens by the holy well at the crossroads and demanded their cloaks or rings or dresses. The maidens said that the robber's eyes were blue as the sea but seemed to be full of tears.

So Janet went to the crossroads, well-dressed in her finest clothes. And there the highwayman leapt out at her, with a 'Stand and deliver! Your green cloak or your finery!'

'Shame on you, Tamlin! Come you home at once,' scolded Janet. 'Do you call this honest work for the Master of Carterhaugh? Come home with me, this instant.'

'Ah, Janet, Janet!' sighed the young man. 'I fear I can never come

home. For I kissed the queen of the fairies, and now for seven years I must obey her every command.'

'Kissed her? Then I'm sure you deserve your fate!' said Janet, flaring up. And she turned her horse and rode back home, her nose sniffy-tilted in the air.

But when her temper cooled, Janet sat down and thought. She sat and thought from Harvest till Hallowe'en, and then she saddled her horse and said goodbye to her mother.

'I must go and rescue Tamlin, for you know how helpless men are to save themselves.'

'Oh, but you'll not go out tonight!' protested her mother. 'Not when the wind is so keen.'

'I have a warm cloak to keep off the wind, mother,' said Janet.

'Oh, but you'll not go out tonight!' begged her mother. 'Not when the rain is so teeming!'

'I have a hood to keep off the rain, mother,' said Janet.

'Oh, but you'll not go out tonight, of all nights!' pleaded her mother. 'Not on All Hallows Eve when all the powers of Hell and Fairyland are out and roaming the world?'

'No other night will do,' said Janet, and kissing her mother she mounted up and rode into the wild, wet, windy night.

She rode to the crossroads where the gallows stood. She braved the ghosts who floated in the misty hollow. She braved the demons who snatched at her skirt out of the long grass. She braved the witches who flitted and twittered across the stormy moon. And she braved the graveyard where dead souls hooted in the trees.

Hiding behind the well, at the crossroads, Janet waited for midnight, when the gates of Fairyland would open and loose the troops of the Fairy Queen to fly about and make mischief.

At last they came, the queen leading the way. Her horse's mane was knotted with silver bells, and her stolen silk petticoats swept the muddy ground. Her company of men was huge—each one young and handsome, each one kidnapped from the sunlit world. Last of all came Tamlin, on a milk-white mare, and the moon glinted on the teardrops in his eyes.

Out sprang Janet, and dragged him from his horse, pulling him to the ground, knotting her white fingers in his rust-red hair. 'Come with me and stay with me,' she said, 'for you are my true-love, Tamlin!'

But the thing in her arms was not Tamlin. In moments, he had changed into a slithering snake which knotted and coiled and writhed all around her.

'Now will you let him go, foolish Janet?' laughed the Fairy Queen.

'Never! You may change him, but my love for him never changes,' and she clung on tight to the snake, though it made her skin crawl with horror.

But the thing in her arms was no longer a snake. Suddenly it had put on feathers and claws, and was slashing at her with a sharp, hooked beak.

'Now will you let him go, foolish Janet?' sneered the queen.

'Never! You may change him, but my love for him never changes!' and she gripped so tight to the vulture that tufts of black feathers came away in her hands.

But the thing in her arms was no longer a vulture. Suddenly it had put on fur and grown into the towering figure of a bear. It hugged Janet to its furry ribs with a strength which all but wrung the life out of her.

'Now will you let him go, foolish Janet?' called the queen.

'Never! You may change him, but my love for him never changes!' and she sank her fingers deep into the bear's fur, so that they looked like two dancers whirling in the moonlight.

But the thing in her arms did not remain a bear for long. It became a lion, a conger eel, a wolf, and a boar. It became a skeleton, a goblin, a dinosaur, and a cackling witch. Even so, Janet refused to let go.

Last and worst of all, the thing in her arms lost all living shape—lost arms and claws and tusks and tail. It thinned to the girth of a spear—cold and rigid—though soon it grew warm in her grip. Tamlin had turned into an iron bar, almost too heavy for Janet to carry. And as she staggered under its weight, the iron bar grew hot, red hot, white hot, singeing her cloak and her hair.

'Drop him! Let him fall, foolish Janet!' shrieked the Fairy Queen. But Janet would not let go her grip on the enchanted Tamlin. Instead she walked with the white hot bar to the brink of the well, and threw it down into the holy water.

There was a mighty hiss of steam.

'Away! Away, your Majesty!' cried Janet. 'Dawn is almost here—the feast of All Hallows—when the angels ride out to hunt the likes of you!'

With a howl of vexation, the Fairy Queen gathered up her reins. 'A curse on you, brave Janet. For you have robbed me of the finest man in my whole company! . . . Away, men! Away!' And the ground shook to the thunder of their galloping hooves as the Enchantress and the Enchanted fled back to Fairyland.

Janet reached down and took her sweetheart's hand. Shivering and sodden, mossy and with frogs in his pockets, Tamlin climbed out of the well. His fairy clothes had fallen into rags, but his hair was still as red as copper and his eyes were still as blue as ever they had been.

'I'll still marry you, though I'm probably a fool to myself,' said Janet, looking him up and down, her hands on her hips. 'But if ever I hear you've been kissing fairies again, I swear I'll take the broom to you and sweep you out of doors! Now, let's get you home before you catch your death of cold.'

And sharing her horse, they rode home.

Now when the young men of Melrose heard what Janet had been ready to do for her sweetheart, they came round her door as eager as bees round a pot of honey. A prince and a chieftain both asked to marry her.

But Tamlin rolled up his sleeves and spat on his hands and said he would fight every man in Scotland before he let his Janet go. For the love he harboured in his heart now would never change—no, not till Fairyland fell into ruins and the hills wore down to sand.

The
Four Friends

I am old,' said the king to his son. 'Before I die, let me see you married, Boy.'

Well, Boy had never thought of marrying before, but he had nothing against the idea. 'All right, father. Who?'

'Go into my art gallery,' said the king. 'There hang portraits of all the unmarried princesses in the world. Choose one, and I will arrange everything.'

It seemed a good way to buy a carriage or a house; not such a good way to choose a wife. But Boy was an obedient son. He took the key from its rack, unlocked the Long Gallery, and walked the length of the room, to and fro, all afternoon. Some were whale-fat, others beanpole-thin. There were ugly, pretty, and pretty ugly princesses; tall ones whose ankles showed, squat ones like pink meringues. There were even some handsome, elegant girls whom the prince studied hard.

But at the end of the room one portrait had been covered—hung with a dust sheet—and there was a notice beneath it which read: LOOK NOT HERE. What would you have done?

So did Boy. He gave the cloth a tug, and down it fell. Then he looked and he looked again. 'You are the one for me,' he said. And the girl in the picture covered her sad face with her hands and turned away. With a series of bangs, all the other portraits fell from the wall, face-down on the carpet.

Boy's father was not angry.

He was heartbroken.

'Why did you have to look where you were forbidden to look?'

'Because she is my Fate, I suppose,' said Boy. 'Who is she?'

'The Princess Perdita—stolen away by the evil sorcerer Chornoy, and kept prisoner by him no-one-knows-where. They call him Sborshchik—The Collector.'

'He collects princesses?'

'He collects the souls of those who try to rescue her and fail! . . . But if Perdita is your Fate, nothing I say will sway you. Take my blessing and go in search of her.' He looked his son fondly up and down—short, short-sighted, and rather short of brains. 'If only you were a boy better framed for Adventure.'

Boy set off. But he did not get far. Before he was out of the palace grounds, he got lost in a wood. Suddenly he fell over the long legs of a man sleeping on the ground.

'Hello,' said the stranger. 'You look like a good man. Will you give me a job?'

'Why, what can you do?' asked Boy.

'Ooo, polish high windows, clear gutters, ford rivers, and so forth.'

'For the right master, I'm sure you would be just the man,' said Boy politely. 'But all I need right now is to get out of this wood.'

'Oh, no prob',' said Long (for that was his name), and he stood up. When he stretched he was so tall that his head stuck up high above the trees.

'The road is that way,' he said. 'I can see it . . . I suppose you wouldn't have a job for a friend of mine?'

Out of his pocket, he drew a small, round man like a football.

'Why, what can he do?'

'Ooo, fence fields, stop draughts, mop up spills and so on,' said Long. 'Show him, Wide.' Wide grinned, broadly.

'To the right master, I'm sure he—' began Boy politely. But Wide was breathing in, growing as he did so.

'Run!' said Long, and without knowing why, Boy ran. Behind them, the empty landscape began to fill up as Wide grew.

First Wide's chest swelled, then his belly, then his head and legs and arms, until just by breathing in, he had grown to the width of a small mountain. With a sigh which blew off Boy's hat, he shrank back to normal size, saying, 'It's an honour to work for you, sir. I suppose you wouldn't have a job for a friend of mine?' Out of his pocket he took a diminutive man in leather shorts and an alpine hat.

'Why is he wearing that blindfold?' asked Boy. 'Is he blind?'

'Not exactly,' said Wide.

'Well, I'm sure to the right master he would be just the man. But all I need right now is to find the Princess Perdita.'

'Easy-peasy,' said the diminutive man (whose name was Quick-Eye). Long stretched up tall and held Quick-Eye in one hand above his head. Quick-Eye took off the blindfold and looked in every direction.

'Without this blindfold, my gaze is so piercing that I tend to set light to things,' Quick-Eye explained. 'Ah yes. There she is. In the Ebony Fortress, among the Hills of Coal, beside the Black Sea. Oh dear, she's crying, poor soul.'

Then Wide put Quick-Eye back in his pocket, and Long put Wide into his pocket and, taking Boy by the scruff of his jacket, set off in the direction of the fortress. His legs were so long that they got there in no time.

A notice was tacked to the door. It said:

> *Let him who would have her, keep her.*
> *Let him who would take her, hold her.*
> *Let him who would try, succeed or DIE!*

'Go in! Go in! Do!' urged a voice behind them. 'The door is not locked.' It was the sorcerer, Chornoy! 'Permit me to show you round my humble home.'

Warily the four friends went inside, and Chornoy led them through his fortress. In every room, on every stair stood strange ebony statues.

'What carving!' exclaimed Boy. 'They could almost be real!'

'They were,' said Chornoy, 'before, like you, they tried to save the princess. There is a forfeit, you see. If you cannot keep the princess by you till morning, you must pay a forfeit.'

Boy gulped. He could see now: the stone figures were frozen in the very act of running or falling, drawing their swords or cowering in fear.

Princess Perdita was even lovelier than her portrait. Her skin was peachy-soft, her mouth as luscious as watermelon, her eyes grape-blue. . . . But she did not move a muscle. Round her waist were three bands of iron without clasp, without padlock, without hinge. And bound by the iron, the princess could neither speak nor move. She looked at Boy with large, imploring eyes which seemed to say, 'Hopeless! It is impossible.'

'Guard her well, young man,' said Chornoy with a heartless snicker. 'Unless I find her here with you in the morning, your soul is forfeit to me, and your body to my collection!'

As night fell, they were left alone in the topmost room of a coal-black tower. As soon as Chornoy was gone, Long took Wide from his pocket, and Wide swelled to the size and shape of the door, to block it. Long wound himself around the tower, to guard it. Boy took hold of Perdita's hand, and they all agreed to keep awake.

Ah, but there was magic at large! By midnight, they were all sound asleep—all except the princess, whose eyes could not close, but whose lips could not speak a warning.

In the morning, to Boy's horror, she had gone! He sat down on the floor and wept. 'I'm done for, and there's nothing to be done.'

'Quick! Quickly, Quick-Eye!' said Long. 'Look and tell us where she is!'

The littlest of the four friends took off his blindfold. There were four windows in the tower, one looking north, one south, one east, one west. From the northern window Quick-Eye could see Chornoy coming, hurrying to claim his forfeit. From the east, Quick-Eye saw the princess.

'Easy-peasy, master. One hundred miles from here is a forest, and in the forest is an oak tree, and in the oak tree is an acorn, and in the acorn is the princess.'

'No prob',' said Long. 'I'll just go and fetch her back.'

And so he did, his long legs covering the ground faster than thought. By the time Chornoy had climbed the winding stair, the princess was hand-in-hand once more with Boy, a sprinkling of oak-leaves in her hair. Chornoy could hardly believe his eyes. With a dull clank, one of the iron bands round the princess's waist fell to the ground, and she was able to move her hands.

'Two nights more you must endure!' raged the sorcerer, then recovering himself he gave a slow, leering smile. 'In the meantime,

gentlemen, do please enjoy the comforts of my home.'

Next night Boy once again sat by the princess and held her hand. Wide stuffed up the doorway, Long encircled the tower, and they all vowed to stay awake. But there was magic afoot, and by midnight they were all snoring (except for the princess whose eyes could not close but whose lips could not speak a warning). In the morning, she was gone.

Boy sat down on the floor and wept. 'Then I'm done for, and there's nothing to be done!'

'Quick! Quickly, Quick-Eye,' said Long.

Quick-Eye ran to the northern window. He could see Chornoy coming, hurrying to claim his forfeit and turn Boy into another statue for his collection. From the east window, Quick-Eye saw nothing, but from the west, he saw the princess.

'Easy-peasy, master. Three hundred miles from here is a mountain, and in the mountain is a rock, and in the rock is a ruby, and in the ruby is the Princess.'

'No prob',' said Long. 'I shall walk there and fetch her back in no time!' and stretching his long legs to the full, he strode off across countryside and moor.

Up the stairs came Chornoy, grinning an evil grin. 'Look your last on the world, fool, for now you have failed—Urghuh!?' He stared in amazement at Boy who sat hand-in-hand with Princess Perdita. With a dull clank, a second iron band round the princess's waist broke and fell to the ground, and she was free to blink her eyes.

'You shan't be so lucky a third time!' Chornoy threatened. 'Enjoy my hospitality while you still may, young man. Tomorrow you will be dead— stone dead!'

That night they tried even harder to stay awake, but there was magic in the air. They nodded, they dozed, they slept. And in the morning the princess was gone.

'Quick! Quickly, Quick-Eye!' said Long. Quick-Eye ran to the northern window. He could see Chornoy coming, skipping and hopping along, laughing and rubbing his hands. But from the east window and the west window, Quick-Eye saw nothing.

Then Boy sat down on the floor and wept. 'I'm done for, and there's nothing to be done.'

'Aha!' said Quick-Eye leaning out of the southern window. 'One thousand miles from here there is a country and in the country is a sea, and in the middle of the sea is a shell and in the shell is the princess.'

'No prob',' said Long, but this time he stuffed Wide into his pocket before striding off across field and moor and mountain with his long legs at full stretch. He reached the sea in no time. But the

sea was so deep! Even Long, at full stretch, could not wade out to the middle without the water closing over his head. 'This is a problem for you, Wide my friend,' he said, and taking the round little man out of his pocket, set him down on the beach.

Wide got down on his hands and knees, put his lips into the rippling waves, and began to drink. He drank till his chest and belly swelled up as big as cathedrals. He drank till his head and his arms and his legs swelled up and he filled the beach like a great, wibbly-wobbling mountain, full of seawater. The sea was now much emptier than before, and Long was able to stride out to the very middle and pick up the shell with the princess inside. It was a long way. Wide began to grunt and groan and turn slightly blue in the face. 'Hurry! Hurry!' said Quick-Eye peeping out of his pocket and beckoning Long. 'He can't hold his breath much longer!'

Long hopped ashore and Wide opened his mouth with an enormous spluttering gurgle.

Out came the seawater, sinking moored boats, scattering shoals of fish, frightening the mermaids. The sea returned to its normal level, and the three friends set off for the Hills of Coal and Chornoy's Ebony Fortress.

But emptying the sea had taken time, and they were one thousand miles from Boy! Peering ahead from amid Long's hair, Quick-Eye said, 'We are never going to get there in time! Chornoy is already climbing the stairs! I do believe we have failed our friend!'

Boy heard the wizard's feet on the stairs and shuddered. He ran to the southern window, but there was no sign of his friends, no sign of the princess. Now he would have to pay the price of failing. Now Chornoy would turn him into a statue.

Chornoy entered, looked all round the room and grinned. 'I did not think you would get her back from there,' he chortled. 'And now the princess is mine, your soul is mine, and your body may join my collection!'

There was a tinkling of glass. Through a pane of the southern window came a tiny sea shell, to land at Boy's feet. It broke open—and there stood . . . the princess! The third iron hoop was already gone from round her waist, and she flung her arms round Boy's neck and kissed him tenderly.

Throughout the Ebony Fortress, the statues stirred and stretched and grumbled sleepily. Scores of princes—angry, vengeful princes—came charging up the stairs of the tower to lay hands on Chornoy. Outnumbered, defeated, Chornoy leapt from a window of the tower and fell into the moat—

just as Long and Wide and Quick-Eye got back from their day out at the seaside.

'When I saw we would not get here in time,' called Long, 'I threw the shell (with Quick-Eye's help). I hope our aim was true?'

'It was, it was!' said the princess, hanging out of the window and blowing kisses to the band of friends. 'Your aim was perfect.'

She had her choice of husbands now, for so many princes had come to try to rescue her from Chornoy's black fortress, and all were now restored to life. Some were very handsome indeed. But she chose Boy, of course, even though he was rather short, rather short-sighted, and rather short of brains. 'You have such nice friends,' she said. 'And you make me laugh.'

The Chase

A wizard (as wizards will) took prisoner a beautiful maiden, wanting to marry her. A young hero (as heroes will) came to rescue her. And with both sharing the one saddle, the two escaped.

But the wizard came after them. Faster and faster he gained on them, closer and closer he came, his purple cloak cracking in the wind, his mouth shouting curious curses.

'I shall stand and fight him!' said the knight boldly.

'Don't be silly. He would turn you into a frog,' said the maiden. 'Seven years I was a prisoner in that wizard's lair, and do you think I sat twiddling my thumbs all that while? I've learned a thing or two about magic.'

So saying, at the next fork in the road, the maiden turned herself into a bucket and the horse into a well. The knight took off his armour, threw it down the well, and leaned over the well wall, so that his head was out of sight.

Up came the wizard in a clatter of hoofbeats and whirl of dust. 'Churl, churl, did you see a knight and a maiden sharing a horse? Which road did they take?'

'Yes, I saw them. They took that road,' said the man with his head down the well, his voice all hollow and echoing.

Away went the wizard. The well changed back into a horse, the bucket into a maiden, and away went they down the other road.

By noon, the wizard realized he had gone wrong somewhere, and doubled back. He picked up their trail at the fork in the road. And being only one-in-the-saddle, he soon caught up with them. Faster and faster he gained on them, closer and closer, his purple cloak cracking in the wind, his mouth mumbling imprecations.

'I shall stand and fight him!' said the knight boldly.

'Don't be foolish. He would turn you into a rat,' said the maiden. 'Seven years I was a prisoner in that wizard's lair, and do you think I sat knitting dishcloths all that while? I've learned a thing or two about magic.'

So saying, at the very next crossroads, she turned the horse into a church and herself into the church bell. The knight (climbing down carefully off the church roof) rummaged in the vestry and found a priest's habit with a big hood.

Up came the wizard in a clatter of hoofbeats and a cloud of dust. 'Priest! Priest! Did you see a knight and maiden sharing a horse? Which way did they go?'

'Bless you, my son, I did! They went north,' said the priest, his face hidden inside his deep hood. Away went the wizard, to the north, and behind him a church bell began to peal out happily.

Then the church turned back into a horse, the bell into a maiden, and the knight took off his priest's habit. Away they went down the road to the south.

By tea-time, the wizard realized he had been tricked, and turned back, picking up their trail at the crossroads. He was angry now, and only one-in-the-saddle. Their horse, by contrast, was feeling not quite itself.

Faster and faster the wizard gained on them, closer and closer, purple cloak cracking in the wind, vowing to be avenged on the knight.

'I must stand and fight him!' said the knight.

'Don't be daft. He would turn you into a Christmas turkey,' said the maiden. 'Seven years I was a prisoner in that wizard's lair, and do you think I sat embroidering tea-cosies all that while? I've learned a thing or two about magic. Get off and lie down on the ground.'

So saying, she turned him into a meadow. Herself she turned into a poppy growing in the meadow.

And the horse she turned into a river of chocolate flowing through the meadow.

Now the wizard was very partial to chocolate. The maiden had not lived seven years in his lair without discovering that. As soon as he saw the river, he jumped down from his horse and began scooping up runny handfuls. Soon his beard was sticky brown, his hair clarted, and his purple cloak smeared with chocolate.

Once or twice he thought of the escaping knight and maiden and got up to leave. But the chocolate was so delicious that he could not resist going back. At last he lay down on the bank and let the chocolate ripples lap into his mouth. He got full and fuller, fat and fatter.

Meanwhile, his horse cropped the grass of the meadow, grazing closer and closer to the blowing red poppy. The poppy trembled in the breath from its snorting nostrils. In a moment, the maiden would have to change herself back or be eaten by the wizard's horse!

Suddenly the wizard gave a groan of pain and pleasure and died of eating too much chocolate. The poppy turned back into a maiden (to the great surprise of the wizard's horse). The meadow turned back into a knight (although his hair had been grazed extremely short) and the river turned back into their own trusty steed.

Now, they had all the time in the world to get home, and they had two horses to ride. That was just as well, mind, because the knight found that his chocolate-brown horse was a good bit smaller than before: his feet trailed along the ground when he mounted up, and the creature's tail was only as long as a bootbrush.

The Frog at
the Well

The queen is sick!'
'The doctors fear for her life!'

'They say she will be dead by morning!'

The queen dead by morning? It was unthinkable. Never had the Highlands seen such a rare and lovely woman as the queen who now lay stretched at the threshold of death.

'Her foot is in the stirrup; she will ride away before morning on Death's black horse,' said the royal physician.

'Her black sail is hoisted; she will sail away before morning to the land from which none return,' said her priest.

'Go? And leave not one word for us?' said her three daughters as they sat and wept by the bed.

The queen opened her eyes and smiled. 'I had a dream just now: it's still so bright before me and loud in my ears. A man all in green . . . "A cup of water from the True Well would heal your sickness," he said.'

'Then I'll go at once to the True Well and bring some back!' exclaimed Prudence, the eldest daughter, jumping to her feet. 'You'll see,' she told her sisters. 'Our mother will be all right after all!' At the bedroom door

she turned back: 'How shall I
find the True Well, Mama?' she asked.

'Follow the great white gull!' whispered
the queen, and spoke not a word more.

As Prudence passed out of the castle
gate, she looked up—and there in the sky
was a big white herring-gull crying as
though its red heart were broken. She
followed it. Over land and brook and
shore and sea she followed it, till, on
an island, she heard the croaking of
a frog.

The frog was seated on a rock
beside a pool of green water which
shone like an emerald. Though
both frog and pond were green, it
has to be said, the frog was not as
pretty as the glittering pond.

'I hoped you'd come,' said the
frog. 'I'm waiting here for a
wife.'

'You'll wait a long time,
with a face like yours,' said
Prudence. 'Would you let
me get by? I need water.'

'Will you marry
me?' asked the frog,
not moving.

'I've no time to spare for fools or frogs. Of course I won't marry you!' said Prudence, offended that such an ugly creature should even ask.

'Then you won't get your water,' said the frog and jumped into the pool with a ploop.

Prudence took no notice. She knelt down on the bank to scoop up water in her blue-glass pitcher. But the water would not be drawn. It soaked away down into its bed until there was no more than a mud-wallow swarming with beetles and snails.

> *'Marry me! Carry me!*
> *Love me or go thirsty!'*

sang a small, cracked voice from somewhere beneath the earth.

But Prudence flung down her blue-glass pitcher and smashed it, saying, 'Never!'

Back at the palace, the queen lay closer to Death than ever. Her eyes were closed, her cheeks were as sunken as a dry pond. Her two younger daughters were frantic for their sister's return—and yet when she came, she had no water—not a drop.

When she told them what had happened, Patience, the second daughter, jumped up. 'I'll go. It takes more than a slimy frog to keep me from what I want!'

Following the great white gull, she crossed land and brook, shore and sea until she too came to the island and the spring, glittering as green as envy. The frog (though it was uglier than she had expected) did not take her by surprise.

'I hoped you'd come,' said the frog. 'I'm waiting here for a wife.'

'So I hear, and here am I, the very wife for you. Just let me draw some water and then we'll be married.'

The frog was so delighted that it somersaulted into the pool crying, 'Marry me, carry me! Marry me, carry me!'

Patience stooped down and filled her red-glass pitcher. This time the magical water did not soak away, but glugged, clear and cool, into the jug. No sooner was it full than Patience leapt up and set off to run, her skirt hitched up into her belt, laughing and yelping with triumph: 'Did you really think I'd marry you, you piece of green slime? Now I've got what I want, you can whistle for a bride—if frogs can whistle. Ha ha ha!'

Back at the palace her sisters were delighted to see her. The queen was more sick than ever, her eyes as circled with dark as the day is, her breathing as hard as if she were under water. 'Don't worry, mother!' cried Patience, darting into the room. 'I've brought you water from the True Well! You'll be singing and laughing again before long!' And she poured the water into a cup and held the cup to the queen's lips.

'Tip it higher!' said Prudence. 'Her lips are not wet.'

'Tip it higher!' said Charity. 'Her lips are not wet.'

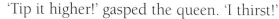

'Tip it higher!' gasped the queen. 'I thirst!'

But though Patience tipped the cup higher and higher, the water shrank down and down in the cup and would not wet the queen's lips. Even when Patience held the cup upside down, not a drop dripped down. She ran to the red-glass pitcher for more water, but when she tipped it up, instead of glug-glug-glug came only the gurk-gurk-groak of a frog's croak. The pitcher was dry.

The queen turned her face to the wall.

'Now I must go to the True Well,' said Charity, the youngest, 'and fetch back some water for Mama. Her wings are spread and she will fly away from us before morning unless I do. Please, Mama! Stay alive until I come back!'

Following the great white gull, she ran across land and brook, shore and sea, until she came, breathless, to the island and the pool as green and shining as a mermaid's eye. There sat the frog on its rock.

'I hoped you'd come,' it said. 'I'm waiting here for a wife.'

'And I will be that wife, if you will have me,' said Charity. Picking up the frog in both hands, she ran with it to the nearest kirk, where a minister (much against his will) declared they were married.

Filling her green-glass pitcher at the pool, and carrying her husband in her apron pocket, Charity ran back over sea and shore, brook and hillside as fast as legs would carry her. But oh! how the tears crammed her throat as her home came into sight. A black flag hung from the flagpole: the queen was already dead.

'Too late! You're too late!' sobbed her sisters, as she set down the pitcher beside the bed. The queen lay there, as white as a gull, no breath between her lips.

From Charity's pocket came the gurk-gurk-groak of a frog's croak. 'Give her the water, wife,' said the frog.

So Charity filled a cup and tipped it against the queen's lips. This time the water did not draw back, but

trickled silvery on to the queen's tongue, and splashed her cheek as well.

With a sigh, the queen turned away from the wall and opened her eyes. 'Thank you. That was the sweetest drink I ever tasted,' she said. 'Why, whatever is the matter, daughters?'

Prudence gulped and Patience hiccuped, and Charity was filled with such joy that she took the frog from her apron pocket and kissed it on its ugly green nose. 'Forgive me, Mama, but since you took ill I have married without your permission. Will you give your blessing to me and my new husband?'

'You didn't!' said Prudence.

'Urgch!' said Patience. 'How could you!'

'Of course,' said the queen sitting up. 'You chose well, my dear. I don't believe I ever saw a more handsome or pleasant-looking gentleman in all my days.'

The sisters stared. It was true. Instead of an ugly green frog, there stood a dashing young man in green velvet, with green eyes, and an emerald in the hilt of his sword.

'I am Prince Ranine,' he said, bowing low to the queen. 'I was enchanted by a witch for ten long years, but your daughter married me and carried me and brought me out of magic. And for that I love her and will do all the days of my life.'

Which pleased Charity, for though she held her mother's life dearer than her own happiness, she had always secretly dreamed of marrying a young and handsome prince.

The Little Mermaid

The waves heaved themselves into the air and fell on the ship like the black flukes of a whale, smashing the aftermast to matchwood. False fire gathered round the mizzen, and the cargo in the hold slid from side to side, like the clapper in a bell. With a dreadful splintering crack, the ship broke its back.

'Abandon ship! She's going under!' called the captain, though his words were snatched away like fish by gulls.

Down on the sea bed, the bells of drowned ships rang a knell for the wreck of another, and the mermaids were stirred from their sleep by the flicker of lightning on the roof of their ocean world. Marina swam to the surface, to sing to the music of the storm. No one sang like Marina.

It was there that she saw him—a young man clinging to a broken spar, eyes shut, hair awash in the creamy foam. She thought he was the most beautiful soul she had seen in all the tides of her saltwater life. Water washed over his face, in and out of his mouth, and she knew that he could not live long in the cold and the violence of the pounding sea. As a wave dragged him off the spar and sank him, she caught him in her gleaming arms and carried him, his head on her breast, away from

the foundering ship, away from danger, all the way to shallow waters and a beach.

With her tail thrashing the soft sand, it was all she could do to roll the young man out of the sea, where he lay, half dead with exhaustion. Waiting for his eyes to open, she planted a single fervent kiss on his lips and said, 'I love you.' Then voices on the cliff path sent her darting under the cover of the waves. Unwilling to leave, she stayed to eavesdrop.

'Look! A sailor lost in the storm!' It was a girl's voice. Running feet crunched down the beach. 'No, not a sailor! Look at his clothes. A prince, surely!'

'Dead?'

'No! No, look! His eyes are opening! Lie still, sir! You are safe! Safe from the sea! Lie still.'

Marina told herself she was glad—that she had saved a prince's life, and that those who loved him would be happy past words. But how could she go back to the bottom of the sea, having seen this sun-kissed land-man, having held him in her white arms, having given her heart to him? He did not even know she existed! With a storm raging within her fiercer than the one which had sunk that ship, Marina swam out towards the morning horizon.

But she returned, time and time again. She returned to the shore where she had left him and, listening to the fishermen working there, mending their nets, learned the name of her prince and the name of his homeland. Time and again she swam to the marble foundations of his seashore castle, to gaze at its fountains, its grand guests. She asked her sisters: 'How can I leave the sea and go to him?'

But her sisters said, 'It's impossible. Forget him. These humans are born and dead in a matter of years. Not like us mer-people.'

'All the more reason I must hurry!' said Marina. 'I must be with him. I would give my hair to be with him!'

'It would cost you more than that,' said her sister unkindly. 'Fishes die out of water.'

But Marina could not forget the prince. She took her courage in both her white hands and swam to the lightless deep-sea trench, to the lair of the Great Sea Witch.

'You come here out of love for a man,' said the Sea Witch, fanning herself with a purple frond of sea coral.

'I do,' said Marina. 'Can you make me a human girl, with legs to run to my love?'

'At a price,' said the Sea Witch. 'Give me your voice, and I shall give you legs.'

Marina put her hand to her throat. In lagoons and reefs, on the backs of turtles and in the wake of whales, she had sung her sweet, mellifluous songs for a century—sung to the strains of harp seals and birds' cries. Her singing was loved and admired by everyone. And without her voice, how would she . . .

'Well? That's the price. Your voice for a human form.'

'I'll pay it,' said Marina. And the next moment she felt a pain in her throat of a crab gouged from its shell, and saw her iridescent tail dissolve in a shower of scales.

'Be sure and win his love, mind,' said the Sea Witch, with a cackle like the crackling of dry seaweed. 'The day he marries another and gives his body and soul to her, yours will dissolve like that tail of yours, into white sea foam.'

The prince was intrigued by the strange girl he found sitting on the harbour steps. Just where he moored his rowing boat and where he liked to fish for dabs, this beautiful, naked girl suddenly appeared one morning, and no one knew where she had come from. She looked at him with such large, affectionate eyes that he felt he must know her from somewhere—could almost remember her from somewhere. And yet, when he asked her her name, where she came from, what she wanted, she said not a word. It was all very mysterious.

Naturally, he took her in—gave her clothes and food and a room in the palace. She was extremely beautiful, and walked with the swaying elegance of a sea flower, and danced more lightly than anyone at court. But not knowing her story, her background, or what she wanted . . . it was a little baffling.

Marina watched her prince like a fish imprisoned in a tank of water, looking out through the glass, gaping soundlessly. She could not tell

him that every step she took burned in the hollow veins of her legs like fire. Instead she smiled and smiled, and hoped that somehow, in time, her love would show in her eyes as clearly as a lighted lamp at a window.

Marina and her prince became inseparable friends. They did everything together, because there was nothing she was not prepared to do. Unlike most of the other young ladies he knew, this one loved to fish, to be out on the water, to climb mountains and to walk in the rain. She also listened when he talked and never did—never could—interrupt.

'I hope our son is not becoming too attached to that strange young woman with the long hair,' said the king.

But the queen reassured him. 'Of course not, my dear. After all, she is only a poor dumb thing. A playmate.'

Sometimes, dangling the fiery agony of her legs in the cool water by the harbour steps, Marina felt a deadly home-sickness for the sea. But she told herself that she had the friendship of her prince, and that was more than voice and tail and sea.

Then he told her of the wedding. 'We're cousins, though we've never met. She was sent to school overseas. Our parents have always wanted the match.'

Marina felt the scream struggle in her throat, powerless to escape. 'You have me!' she wanted to say. 'Marry me! Why not me?' But her voice was tightly sealed in a clam-shell on the barnacled shelves of the Sea Witch's cave, and she could not make him understand.

'You know,' said the prince, 'there's only one girl I shall ever love, whoever they find me for a bride.'

Marina's heart swelled and ached with happiness. It was enough. She was loved. And the souls of those who love one another are together for ever when they die, aren't they?

'Yes,' said the prince. 'It was before you and I met. I was shipwrecked one stormy night, and when I woke on the beach and opened my eyes, there was a girl looking down at me—a beautiful girl. She cared for me until I was fit to travel home—but who she was I'll probably never know . . . Oh! Whyever are you crying, little friend?'

It's not fair. It's not fair. It's not fair. The words beat at her brain like a hammer. If he had woken a moment earlier, the face he saw would have been hers. Marina felt robbed, cheated—as though the girl on the beach had deliberately stolen away her every hope of happiness. Marina drew a deep, trembling breath. But I am here, and she is not, she thought. And that makes it all worthwhile.

As the wedding came closer, the prince became more and more uneasy. 'I do declare,' he said, 'if I can't love this cousin of mine, I shan't go through with the marriage. I shan't. I shall marry you, instead!'

They even travelled together by ship to the wedding. And in the ship's wake, Marina saw her sisters swimming, beckoning, begging her to leap overboard and join them. Their song came over the water, as sharp as starlight in Marina's ears: 'Come away! Come away! Leave the world of men! Before it's too late!'

But Marina knew that it was already too late. She belonged to the world of men because her heart belonged to a man-of-the-dry-land. It was live or die, love or perish.

Die, she thought, when she saw the prince's face. He had just glimpsed

his bride—and the bride was none other than the girl on the beach; the one who had won his love with nothing more than a smile. Marina had to admit, the princess was very beautiful. She was ashamed of the words hammering against her brain: It's not fair. It's not fair. It's not fair.

That night, Marina stood on the deck of the ship, her legs on fire, her heart ragged with regret. So. She must die with the sunrise. The prince's heart was given to another girl, and Marina's must dissolve into sea foam. For this she had deserted her own kind. For this she had given up the turquoise pools, the whalesong, the halls of pearl and scarlet coral. For this the Sea Witch had gashed her tail into feeble little legs, silenced her singing.

The bridal tent stood billowing on the deck, golden pennons stirring, small silver bells jingling in the breeze. Inside slept the prince and his bride. The sea kissed the hull of their ship.

Up through the waves came five strange, seal-like heads, whitely grotesque in the moon. It was her sisters, their heads shaved, their eyes big with shock. Something glinted in the moon: a long knife with a curved blade. 'We sold our hair to the Great Sea Witch to buy this! Kill the prince before morning and you needn't die! You shall have back your tail! There are centuries more life waiting for you in the sea. Hurry, little sister!'

Their kindness moved her to tears. 'Oh thank you! Thank you, my

dear, dear sisters!' she mouthed into the wind. The long knife arced through the air and rattled on the deck at her feet. She snatched it up and ran—oh, the pain of running!—to lift the flap of the bridal tent.

There lay the prince, his bride's head on his chest, his hands full of her hair. One blow, and Marina would be free of her disastrous bargain, free of pain, free to live! The sharp rim of the sun was just cutting the wire of the horizon. Her blood seemed already to be turning to sea foam. She folded her two hands round the hilt, kissed the blade . . .

. . . and flung the knife away over the ship's rail. Kill her prince? Not for a world of sea treasure, not for a million years of joy. Climbing a short way up the rigging, she threw herself headlong into the sea, feeling, even as she fell, her heart and body flaking into foam.

And yet she never touched the waves. Her sisters, clutching each other in horror as they saw the precious knife thrown overboard, looked in vain for the droplet fragments of their dead sister; the sea was as smooth as gunmetal and there was not one fleck of foam. Then one mermaid shouted, and the others looked where she was pointing. There in the brightening sky, above the rosy clouds of morning, was the flicker of white wings. Gulls? No.

On board ship, the prince woke with strange misgivings and began searching for his little friend—calling, growing anxious. Fearing she had fallen overboard, he gazed down into the sea, not up into the sky, of course, or he might have glimpsed the angel, new-made by God to watch over him and his bride and his unborn children and his children's children. Wherever such a quantity of love is found in one heart— whether it is a mermaid's or a human heart—there are the makings of an angel. So before the long-bladed knife had even fallen to the ocean bed, Marina had regained her voice and was, to her great astonishment, singing among choirs of angels in the turquoise steeples of the sky.

Hansel and Gretel

Their father loved Hansel and Gretel very much. Perhaps that is why their stepmother hated them so, wanting all his love for herself. But since she ruled the household with her nagging tongue, she knew she could find a way to be rid of them. When the famine began she said to her husband, 'There's not enough food to keep us two alive, let alone those worthless children of yours. Take them into the forest with you tomorrow, and see to it that they . . . lose their way there.'

Luckily, little Gretel was lying awake, too hungry to sleep. She heard what her stepmother said. 'Wake up, Hansel!' she whispered. 'Our mother means to kill us!'

When Hansel heard about the plan, he soothed his sister's crying and crept out of bed. In the moonlit garden he filled his pockets with all the white stones he could find, then crept back to bed and tried to sleep . . . though who could sleep with such a day ahead?

Their unhappy father was a woodcutter and each day went deep into the forest to work. That day he took his children with him and led them, down mazes of tangling pathways, to a clearing in the very middle of the woods. 'Wait here for me,' he said, kissing them and wiping tears from his eyes. 'I'll come back for you at home-time—God forgive me if I don't.' They could hear his axe-blows—thud, crack—echoing further and further off. Then silence settled on them like leaves.

When night fell they were all alone—abandoned, lost. Gretel began to cry. 'Don't fret,' said Hansel. 'You know those stones I gathered last night? As we came here this morning I dropped them one by one. All we have to do is wait for the moon to rise.'

And sure enough, the rising moon, like a lighthouse casting its beam across a black sea, shone on the forest and lit the white stones Hansel had dropped. They shone out like gems, guiding the children to the very front door of their cottage. Knock knock. The look on their father's face when he opened the door was like Christmas morning. The look on their stepmother's face was Hallowe'en.

When the children were safely tucked up in
bed, they could hear the bark and snarl of her,
as she nagged her husband. 'You fool! Trust
you to let them find their way home! You'd
better make a better job of it tomorrow, or we'll
both starve!'

Gretel clutched her brother's hand in terror,
but he soothed her sobbing. Instead of eating
the crust of bread given him as supper, Hansel
pushed it deep into his pocket.

Next day, as the woodcutter led them down miles of tangling
pathways into the very middle of the woods, Hansel picked from the
crust crumb after crumb of bread, dropping a trail of breadcrumbs,
marking the way they had come. In the heart of the forest their father
kissed them and dried his eyes. 'Wait here for me. I shall come back for
you at home-time. God forgive me if I don't.' They could hear his
axe-blows—thud, crack—echoing further and further off. Then
silence fell, and Gretel began to cry.

Hansel was not worried. He even whistled as he waited. He
knew their father would not come back for them. But he
also knew that the white breadcrumbs would shine out in
the white moonlight, and show them the way home to
their front door.

Daylight faded. The woodcutter did not come.
The moon rose . . . And all the little birds of the
forest went home to their nests with white bread
in their beaks for their hungry chicks. When
Hansel and Gretel began to look for the path

home, every moonlit path looked the same; there was no way to tell them apart. The birds had eaten every crumb. Hansel and Gretel searched and ran and called, but they were alone in the heart of the great forest, lost, hopelessly lost.

Huddling together for warmth, the children slept. And the birds, realizing what they had done, dropped a blanket of leaves over the sleeping pair, a quilt of green and yellow.

Next day the children began walking aimlessly through the forest, searching for berries to eat. They were fearfully hungry. So both thought they were dreaming when, in a sunlit clearing, they saw a funny little cottage.

Its walls were made of gingerbread, its roof of marzipan. Its shutters were wafers, its door chocolate, each chimney a twist of barleysugar. Hansel and Gretel rushed up a path cobbled with sugared almonds and raced around the delightful house, sniffing and stroking the walls, trampling flowerbeds of parma violets without even realizing. Hansel broke a piece off the roof and crammed it into his mouth.

'Oho! Rats in the eaves, eh? Nibble my house, would you! Well, you'll be sorry . . . !' Out of the house scuttled a bent, gnarled old woman, her face as crumpled as a ball of paper. But peering short-sightedly at the visitors, she showed her yellow teeth in a twisted smile. 'Children, is it? Well, how nice. Help yourselves, little ones. Do! There's better inside. Won't you come in and dine?'

In went Hansel and Gretel: 'We're very sorry! We were just so hungry, and all those delicious—'

'Not another word,' said the old lady, sitting them down at table. 'Here's caramel for you, boy, and limedrops for you, my dear.' And she brought so many plates of sweets to the table that the children groaned with pleasure.

It was a strange kitchen, with a big stove and table, the rest of the room bare but for a large cage in one dark corner and a large locked chest in another. 'Now who's good at housework?' asked the old lady, as they sat loosening their belts. At once Gretel jumped up.

'I am! Shall I wash up, Grandma?' she asked.

'You will!' Suddenly, with a cackle that shattered the water jug, the old woman knocked over Hansel's chair, spilling him on to the floor. With a twig broom, she pushed him into the cage and clanged shut the door before throwing the broom at Gretel's head.

'And when you've done the dishes you can sweep the floor and make my bed—scrub the step and feed the chickens! From today onwards, you're my slave! House-breakers! Roof-nibblers! You're the lucky one, girl! Your brother won't live as long!'

Hansel rattled the bars of the iron cage. 'Why?! Let me out! What are you going to do to me?'

The old witch hobbled over to him and peered through the bars. Her lips drooled. 'Well, EAT you, of course, boy!' she croaked. 'As soon as you're fat enough!'

Naturally, thanks to the famine, Hansel and Gretel were about as thin as two children could be. But the old witch (who liked only meat, and plenty of meat on the bone) had a remedy for that. Every day she served Hansel a delectable meal of sweet things, fattening him up for the day she would roast him and eat him with a sprig of parsley in his hair.

Being short-sighted, she bumped about the house breaking off pieces of candy and fumbling them on to a plate which she tipped through the bars of the cage, showering Hansel with sugar. Then, 'Put out your finger, boy!' she would yelp, and squeezing his finger fiercely between her toothless gums, she would spit with disgust and say, 'Too thin! Too thin! Not ready yet!'

Oddly enough, Hansel's finger grew no fatter. Shall I tell you why? It was Gretel's idea. 'Whenever the witch says, "Put out your finger!"' she whispered to him one night, 'hold out this stick instead.' And she gave him a thin twig from the kindling beside the stove. So no matter how much the witch fed Hansel, the 'finger' she mumbled each day between her toothless gums grew no fatter than a twig, and away she would go, saying, 'Too thin! Too thin! Will this boy never be fat enough to eat?'

Inside his cage, plump, round Hansel sat and watched his sister work her fingers to the bone doing the witch's housework while he ate and slept and thought of the day when the trick with the twig stopped working.

'Enough!' screeched the witch one morning. 'I've waited long enough. I haven't eaten roast boy now for a year, and I have a mind to eat some today! Gretel! Light the stove!'

Now the stove was huge—a cast-iron cave of a cooker, with a grate deep at the back which had to be lit by hand. The witch gave Gretel a lighted spill and told her, 'Crawl inside and light the stove, girl, and be quick about it!'

'I don't know how,' said Gretel.

'Just crawl inside and light the kindling, you stupid child!' said the witch.

'I don't understand, ma'am,' said Gretel.

'Why not? It's as easy as spitting!' raged the old witch.

'I'm very stupid,' said Gretel. 'Stepmother always said so.'

'Must I do everything myself!' exclaimed the witch in exasperation, and snatched the spill from Gretel. Stretching her scrawny neck and poking her goat-like head in at the door of the oven, she reached forward and lit the kindling.

With a single blow of her broom, Gretel whacked the witch's black behind with all her might, toppling her into the oven and slamming shut the cast-iron door. The fire in the oven blazed and roared. The witch burned with a purple flame. The gingerbread ceiling softened and sagged in the heat, and both chimney pots fell to the ground outside.

Meanwhile, Gretel fetched the keys from under the witch's mattress, and freed Hansel: he could barely squeeze through the cage door, he was so fat. Inside the locked chest they found a fortune in pearls and jet and gold—none of it made of sugar.

So with one sack full of gingerbread and one of treasure, the two children set off back through the forest. They had no idea which way to go, but came soon to a wide river where swans as large as Venetian gondolas cruised up and down, up and down.

'Will you carry us over?' called Gretel, and one swan drew close to the bank, allowing the children to nestle down between its folded wings.

Down the river, riding the current, went the great white swan until, at last, Hansel recognized the countryside around him. 'I know where we are! We could be home in an hour!'

The swan set them ashore, and Hansel and Gretel walked the rest of the way to their own front door, dragging their heavy sacks. But there was something strange about the ramshackle old cottage, something different. It was silent. No shrill carping or complaining disturbed the birds from the roof-ridge. No noise of nagging unsettled the butterflies from the flowers. Their stepmother was nowhere around.

When their father opened the door, he hugged his lost children so close they could not speak. 'I thought you were dead! I thought I'd killed you! I haven't had a minute's peace since I gave in to that cruel, wicked woman! I should never have listened to her! Can you ever forgive me? She's gone now! Dead and gone, and good riddance, I say! Come inside, come inside! I'll find you something to eat—something, somehow . . .'

But there was no need for the woodcutter to sacrifice his last bite of bread. For Hansel and Gretel had brought a sackful of gingerbread to eat, and gold to buy meat and bread and more. And with the death of the witch, deep in the forest, the famine left that part of the world—spread its wings and flew away like a great black crow, leaving the fields full of grain once more and the cows as brown as gingerbread . . . and almost as fat as Hansel.

The Tinderbox

There was once a leaf trembling on a twig, the twig on a branch, the branch on a tree, the tree by a road, and under the tree—a big fat witch in an apron.

Along the road came a soldier, as thin and sharp-nosed as the bayonet on his rifle. 'Hoi! Young man! How would you like to be as rich as now you are poor?' called the witch.

'What must I do? Marry you?' said the soldier. His mother had warned him not to speak to strange women, and this was as strange as any he had ever met.

'This tree is hollow. But it's thin, too, and I am fat,' said the witch. 'Now you, you're as thin as a hair; I could thread you through the eye of a needle and mend my socks. So climb down the tree and fetch me something from the cavern below.'

'Why? What's down there that you want so badly?' asked the soldier, whose name was Tommy.

'I want a tinderbox that lies in the third room. Bring me that and you can help yourself to anything else you find down there. Here, tie this rope round your waist and I'll lower you down. Take my apron, too.'

'I have to cook?' said Tommy, holding the apron at arm's length between finger and thumb.

'The three rooms are guarded by three dogs. No, don't worry. They won't hurt you if you sit each dog on this apron. Hurry now! Or do you want to be poor all your life?'

Tommy was curious to see inside the tree. More out of curiosity than greed, he jumped into its branches and slipped down inside the hollow trunk, knapsack on his back and the witch's apron and rope round his waist.

It was a long way down, and dark. A ferocious barking came up the narrow flue and, as his feet touched ground and he struck a match, he was confronted by a dog.

Did I say dog? It was as big as a lion, with eyes as large as saucers. Quickly Tommy whipped off the apron and laid it down, then—'Steady now—I've got you!—Don't wriggle!'—sat the dog on the apron. Quiet as a tea cup, the dog sat and stared at Tommy with its huge eyes, while Tommy stared around him, his eyes almost as big. Everywhere he looked, he saw the red glint of copper. There were copper coins spilling out of barrels, chests, and baskets.

This is some robber's lair, he thought, cramming his pockets and knapsack with such a weight of coins that his knees bent. Nudging the dog off the apron, he went on into the second room, just as the match between his fingers fizzled out. He had no sooner struck a second match than he was confronted by a second dog.

Did I say dog? It was as big as a horse, with eyes as large as dinner plates. Tommy laid down the apron then—'Oof!—If you'd just—shift over—ow, my back!'—got the dog on to the apron. Quiet as a dinner table, the dog sat and stared at Tommy with its gigantic eyes, while Tommy stared around him, his eyes almost as big. Everywhere he looked he saw the thin gleam of silver. There were silver coins spilling out of crates, vases, and panniers.

This is some pirate's treasure, he thought, emptying his pockets and knapsack of copper to fill them with silver. He picked up such a weight of silver that he bowed at the knees. Then, leaning against the huge dog, he got it off the apron and went on into the third room, just as his match went out.

He had no sooner struck another than he backed straight out of the

room again. For it was almost full of dog. Wall-to-wall dog: a beast as
vast as an elephant, with eyes as large as cartwheels and a bark like a
thundercrack. Tommy waved the apron at it like a flag of surrender,
then—'Go on!—uugh!—move yourself!—Ooof!—Go on, you brute!'—
barged and shifted the monumental dog on to the apron.

Quiet as a wagon, the dog sat and stared at Tommy, its vast eyes
slowly revolving, while Tommy stared around him, his eyes nearly as
big. Everywhere he looked, he saw the sunny sparkle of gold. There
were gold coins covering the floor, piled against the walls, spilling out
of sacks and trunks and troughs.

This is some wizard's fortune, thought Tommy. No ordinary man
carried all this here. And he emptied his pockets and knapsack of silver,
to refill them with gold. Just before his match went out, he noticed a
cheap tin tinderbox lying on the floor and picked that up, too.

The witch's rope was tugging at his waist now. Her fat voice came
oozing through the darkness: 'What's keeping you? Where are you?
Hurry up! Have you found it?' Tommy let her pull him up from the
cavern; up the hollow tree until he could wriggle out on to a branch.
'Did you get it?' she demanded. 'Did you get the tinderbox? Did you?'
Jumping up and down in a frenzy.

'What can it do? Why do you want it so much?' asked Tommy.

'Give! Give it! Give! Give! Give!' screamed the witch, clawing at his
dangling boots. Unfortunately, she pulled so hard that she dislodged
him from the branch. He fell, knapsack and all and, like a rock falling
on a beetle, squashed the fat witch flat.

She was quite dead. There was nothing for Tommy to do but go
whistling on his way into town.

What a popular man he was when he got there! He bought drinks,

he lent loans, he gave gifts, he kept open-house, inviting everyone to dinner who cared to come. He bought the most fashionable clothes, saw the most fashionable plays, betted on the prettiest horses at the racetrack. In no time at all he had a thousand dear friends who loved him like a brother.

Every day they talked about the same thing, those fine gentlemen. They talked about Princess Blaise— whom no one had ever seen—guessing what she looked like, guessing her age, guessing whom she might marry. It did not seem very likely to Tommy that Blaise would ever marry anyone. For she lived in a tower of copper, safe from spying eyes, by order of the king. 'What I'd give to see that princess!' said Tommy, but then all his dear friends said the same.

And then the money ran out.

In no time, Tommy's stomach was as empty as his knapsack. His landlord turned him out of his luxury lodgings, and his dear friends melted away like the morning frost. He found himself back in the wood, sheltering under a tree, with nothing to his name but one fashionable suit, a gun, a knapsack, and a cheap tin tinderbox. Breaking twigs from the dead trees, he built himself a fire to keep warm by, and struck his last match to light it. The match went out.

Now, the right and proper purpose of a tinderbox is to strike sparks and light fires. So that's what Tommy did. At least that is what he started to do.

No sooner did he strike a spark than through the wood came bounding and barking the dog from the cavern, its eyes as large as saucers. 'Whaadawaant, master?' it barked.

'Oho, is that how it goes!' said Tommy and struck the tinderbox twice. Two sparks, and through the woods came bounding and barking the dog with eyes as large as dinner plates.

'Whaadawaant, master?' it barked.

'So that's why the fat witch wanted the tinderbox,' said Tommy and struck three times. Three sparks, and through the wood came bounding and barking, felling trees like a stampede of elephants, the dog with eyes as big as cartwheels.

'Whaadawaant, master?'

'I see now that I am the richest man in the kingdom,' said Tommy to the dogs. 'Let's start with a sack of gold, if you would be so kind.' The dogs fetched what he wanted instantly.

* * *

Rich once more, Tommy took fine lodgings again in town. But this time he did not think of parties or fashionable clothes, of making himself popular or making himself famous. He just thought of the Princess Blaise. Striking the tinderbox once, he summoned the dog with eyes as large as saucers.

'Whaadawaant, master?' barked the dog.

'I wish to see the princess from the copper tower,' said Tommy. 'Is that possible?'

Away went the dog, as fast as thought, and back it came. Stretched out along its back, sound asleep and dreaming, lay the Princess Blaise, her coppery hair hanging down. Tommy stared and stared. She was so beautiful that he could not help but kiss her. Then, ashamed of himself, he told the dog to carry her safely back to bed before she woke.

*   *   *

'I had the strangest dream last night,' said Princess Blaise to her parents. 'I dreamt a dog with eyes as big as saucers carried me down to the town, and there a soldier with eyes like stars kissed me.' And she sighed, as if to say, 'Sweet dreams.'

'How nice, dear,' said the queen. But her fist tightened on her teaspoon and her teeth ground on her toast. 'I don't care for such dreams,' she told the king later. 'Let's set a maid to keep watch over our dear darling daughter.'

All day, Tommy could think of nothing but the princess. Next night he struck the tinderbox and asked the dog with eyes as large as saucers to fetch the princess to him again.

Away went the dog, as fast as thought, and home it came, the sleeping princess on its back. This time Tommy gave her two kisses, and stared till his eyes felt as big as dinner plates.

Little did he know that a maid had been keeping watch over the lovely princess. What a fright that dog had given her! But she was a brave girl, and when the dog carried the princess away through the open window, she hitched up her nightdress and ran after it, all the way to town.

Seeing the house to which the dog ran, the maid said to herself, 'All these houses look the same. How will the king's soldiers find this one in the morning and arrest this vile kidnapper?' Clever girl that she was, she took out a piece of chalk and drew a cross on Tommy's door.

Later that night, Tommy sighed one more sigh and told the dog to carry his beloved princess back to her bed. Luckily, the dog's huge eyes gave it the sharpest sight. As it looked to left and right, it saw the chalk cross on the door. And just as if that dog had gone to school all its life and learned the alphabet up to X, it took out a piece of chalk and drew crosses on every other door in the street—every other door in the town.

* * *

The king's troopers came back from town glum and empty-handed. 'Well? Did you arrest him?' demanded the king. 'Did you find the house with the cross on the door?'

'We found a hundred houses with crosses on the door,' said the sergeant-major.

Well, the poor maid almost lost her head. 'If you please, your Majesty,' she begged, 'give me one more chance and I'll find him out for you, the kidnapper! I know how it can be done! Just sew a silk purse to the princess's nightdress—a purse with a little hole in it—and fill the purse with buckwheat.'

When, on the third night, Tommy sent his dog to fetch the sleeping princess from her bed, no one followed his bounding down to town. There was no need. The buckwheat trickled, grain by golden grain, down from the silk purse, and left a trail on the moonlit ground. Though Tommy took from the princess no more than three kisses, and though he soon returned her unharmed to her bed, the royal guard came pounding on his door at dawn and dragged him away to prison in his nightshirt.

'He shall hang in the morning!' vowed the king.

* * *

Through his prison bars, Tommy could see the scaffold. He could see, too, the distant glimmer of the copper tower, could see the stars setting on the last night of his life. He was very afraid.

A little boy kicked a fir cone across the prison yard. Tommy knew by the sharpness of his nose that the boy was hungry. 'Psst! Psst, boy! How would you like to be as rich as now you are poor? Run to my lodgings and fetch me the tinderbox lying on the table. You can help yourself to anything else you find there.'

Behind him a key rattled in the lock, and in came the jailer holding a noose of rope. 'Yer wanted, sir,' he said. 'At the gallows.'

The king and queen were there to see the execution. Drums rolled, people stared, their eyes as big as gold coins, as the prisoner was led out to the scaffold. At the last moment, a little boy darted through the crowd and thrust a cheap tin tinderbox into the hand of the condemned man.

'May I smoke a last pipe before I die?' said Tommy to the king. 'It's not much to ask.' The king nodded.

One—one two—one two three times, Tommy struck a spark.

Bounding and barking, over market and river, over coaches and platoons of soldiers, over houses and shops, came all three dogs, eyes whirling and blazing in their heads, their steamy breath clouding the cold morning air. They bit through the gallows, they tossed the executioner over the church. They licked the queen and picked up the king by his gown.

And if Tommy had been a worse-tempered man, who knows what his dogs might have done at his command.

You have no idea how popular Tommy became all of a sudden. 'Hurrah for Tommy!' shouted the terrified crowd, as the three dogs tore round and round them. 'We want Tommy for Prince! Three cheers for Tommy!' All thoughts of hanging him were forgotten, and the king and queen vowed they had never met a more suitable bridegroom for their dear, darling daughter.

But Tommy did not use his magic dogs to scare the princess into marrying him. He did not need to. She said, 'You remind me of someone I met in a dream. It was a sweet dream. I liked you then and I like you now.'

It is lucky she liked dogs, too, because all three came to the wedding, bounding and barking ahead of the golden coach, then lolling on the church steps, staring and staring and staring.

Cap-o'-Rushes

A weary old king took it into his head to retire and to split his kingdom between his three daughters. But which of them should have the fat green lands to the south, which the bare bleak mountains to the west, which the purple wilds of the north? He could have tossed a coin to decide. But being a vain man he asked each girl instead: 'How much do you love me?'

'More than gold and silver,' said Goneril, his oldest daughter, wanting the best share.

'More than diamonds and rubies,' said Regan, trying to outdo her.

The king purred with pleasure. 'And you, Cordelia?' he asked his favourite daughter. 'How much do you love me?'

'As much as meat loves salt,' said the little princess.

'What's that supposed to mean?' said the king scowling. 'Speak again.'

But the youngest would say nothing more. The king, who had always thought she loved him best of all, threw a terrible tantrum, tossing furniture about and shouting: 'If I mean so little to you, you can just get out! Go on! Get out! And don't come back! I'll split my kingdom between Goneril and Regan. As for you, you can walk the world and starve for all I care! Meat? Salt? Heartless, thankless child!'

So Cordelia went out into the stormy world, taking with her only three dresses of her dead mother's, as remembrances. She picked rushes from the river bank and wove herself a cap and cloak, such as beggars wore to keep off the rain and cold. And she threw her name into the river, so afterwards people had no name to call her by but 'Cap-of-Rushes'.

If she was ever to eat again, she had to find work. So she knocked at the door of a royal castle in the kingdom next door. 'I would work hard for no pay and only a bite to eat and somewhere to lay down my head,' said Cap-of-Rushes.

'Then you may scrape pots and shine pans in the kitchen,' said the housekeeper, 'and sleep by the stove at nights.'

The little princess was as good as her word. She worked hard from dawn till dark, though her soft hands were not used to scrubbing. She was so helpful and so hard-working that she had soon earned a place for herself in the castle kitchen—in the hearts of the other servants, too. They told her all their troubles and all their news, and she always cheered them up with her kindness and her good advice.

So when the king announced that he was to give a party, with dancing and feasting and orchestras and a hundred guests, the word soon reached the little scullery maid.

'Oh, Cap-of-Rushes! Cap-of-Rushes! It's going to be such a grand affair! Three days of dancing! One, two, three!'

'The king and the prince and all the dukes and duchesses will be there!'

'Everyone in the kingdom is invited! And we shall serve the food and take the cloaks and wait at table and see it all, Cap-of-Rushes . . . though you'll have to find something better to wear than that cape of yours!'

'It sounds grand,' said Cap-of-Rushes, nothing more.

But on the day of the first ball, she said she was too tired to go upstairs and watch the dancing. So the other servants left her asleep in front of the stove and went without her.

As soon as they were gone, Cap-of-Rushes opened her eyes, fetched out her bundle, and took off her coarse cape and cap. She put on a dress of her mother's—a white dress stitched all over with pearls—and brushed her hair until every tangle was out. Then she ran upstairs to join in the dancing.

* * *

'Cap-of-Rushes! Oh, Cap-of-Rushes, you should have been there!' The servants and footmen and maids and cooks all tumbled into the kitchen, noisy with

excitement. The little scullery maid asleep in front of the stove blinked her eyes and sat up.

'There was this princess—oh! she was lovely!'

'A white dress . . .'

'The prince couldn't take his eyes off her!'

'How they danced!'

'How they talked!'

'She just left—not ten minutes ago!'

'Oh, Cap-of-Rushes, such an amazing evening!'

Cap-of-Rushes pulled her grassy cape closer around her. 'It must have been grand,' she said, but nothing more.

Next evening the music began again upstairs in the grand ballroom. All the servants changed into their best livery, but Cap-of-Rushes said she was too tired to do anything but sleep, and lay down in front of the stove.

As soon as they were gone, she changed her ugly cape and cap for a second dress—a black one sewn with diamonds like the night sky— and brushed her hair till it floated around her head as she ran upstairs.

Once again she danced all night with the prince and this time it was not so easy to slip away, for she could hardly bear to part from the prince, nor he from her. Even so, she was back in front of the stove before her friends burst excitedly into the room.

'Cap-of-Rushes! Oh, Cap-of-Rushes, you should have been there! That princess came again.'

'A black dress covered in diamonds!'

'The prince loves her for sure!'

Cap-of-Rushes pulled her grassy cape closer around her. 'It must have been grand,' she said, but nothing more.

 On the third evening, she again pretended she
was too tired to go to the ball, and the others
again went without her. As soon as they were
gone, she put on her third dress—a red one sewn
with rubies—and brushed her hair till it crackled
with electricity. She could hardly wait to see the prince, for
her love for him was big like a pain inside her.

As they danced, he asked to marry her—said he would die if he could
not marry her—seized her hand and slipped his own ring of state on to
her finger. But when Cap-of-Rushes looked into his eyes, she saw her
own reflection and thought: what am I? A scullery maid, cast out by my
father. When he finds out, the prince, too, will hate me. Wriggling free
of his grasp, Cap-of-Rushes fled.

'Don't go!' cried the prince. 'Friends! Servants! Stop her for me,
please! I mustn't lose her!'

Guests and guards, servants and maids scattered in every direction.
Cooks and footmen tumbled down the back stairs into the kitchen, as
fast as they could go . . . but found no one—only the little scullery maid
asleep in front of the stove.

'Oh, Cap-of-Rushes! Cap-of-Rushes! Such a calamity! Wait till
you hear!' wailed the head cook. (They did not realize that
underneath that nasty cape of reeds rustled a gorgeous gown of red
silk and rubies.)

Though riders galloped throughout the land, no trace could be found
of the girl in the scarlet dress. And when it seemed she was gone forever,
the prince cancelled all his royal engagements and stayed in his rooms,
day after week after fortnight.

'Oh, Cap-of-Rushes! Cap-of-Rushes!' sobbed the cook, as she

chopped onions one day. 'I'm afraid this is the last meal I shall ever cook for that poor young man!'

'What poor young man is that?' asked Cap-of-Rushes.

'I'm not supposed to say. It's a state secret,' said the cook, biting her lip. 'But the king sent for me this morning and told me to cook soup for the prince. Seems he won't eat, can't sleep. He's pining away with a broken heart.'

When Cap-of-Rushes heard that, she said, 'Let me make the soup. Please.' And as she prepared it, she slipped the ring of state into the serving dish.

The soup was sent up to the prince. At first he said he would not drink it, but at last the queen persuaded him to take one sip. And lo and behold! there in his spoon was the ring.

'LET THE COOK BE SENT FOR!'

The cry echoed down the back stairs. The cook quaked in her shoes. 'What have I done? Why me?' The footmen and maids gaped back at her and shrugged helplessly. So, wiping her trembling hands on her apron, the cook went to the prince's bedside and curtsied.

'Who cooked this soup?' the prince demanded to know, his face as pale as Death.

Thinking the soup was bad, and that poor little Cap-of-Rushes would get into trouble, the kind-hearted cook said, 'I did, your honour, if it please you, thank you kindly like.'

'No!' said the prince, bounding out of bed and advancing on the cook with the bowl outstretched in his hands. 'WHO COOKED THIS SOUP? TELL ME THE TRUTH.'

'Oh mercy!' cried the cook, putting her apron over her head. 'It was Cap-of-Rushes, your honour! But she's really such a good girl, if you just knew her!'

'Send her to me,' said the prince, and this time his voice was soft and gentle, because he knew he had found his missing princess.

When Cap-of-Rushes went to the prince's room it was not in her cape and cap of woven reeds. To the amazement of all the kitchen staff, she took that off and burned it on the stove, revealing a dress beneath of scarlet silk sewn with rubies. When the prince saw her, he knew he need not die; and when Cap-of-Rushes saw her prince, she suddenly knew how she could marry him after all and be happy evermore.

* * *

'Goneril! Regan! We are invited to a wedding in the kingdom next-door,' said the weary old king one morning. He had no wish to go—had rather lost his taste for parties and jollifications. But of course he could not refuse. So he and his daughters travelled to the wedding, and a very lavish affair it was, too.

The wedding feast covered seventeen trestle

tables—roast swan and quail and golden pheasant, roast beef and pork, lamb and venison, besides all the rolls and pâtés and pastries. More than a hundred guests stood up to toast the bride—(everyone said that behind that cloud of snowy veil she was a tremendous beauty). Then the serious business of eating began. Hands reached, forks glittered, teeth sank into the delectable fare. But ten minutes later everyone had lain down their forks.

The food was uneatable.

It tasted of nothing. The cooks had forgotten to use any salt!

It was embarrassing, yes. It was disappointing, true. Guests muttered between themselves that the head cook ought to be hanged. But even so! It was surely nothing to cry about! So why was the old retired king from the kingdom next-door sobbing as if his heart would break, face sunk in his hands, the tears running out between his fingers, dripping on to his uneaten meat? 'Whatever is the matter?' they asked him.

'I had . . . I had a daughter once,' wept the old man. 'I asked her how much she loved me and she said— oh, God forgive me!—she said, "As much as meat loves salt". I was so stupid that I threw her out into the stormy world to starve and die. It's only now—too late—I understand: she really loved me best of all!'

But before the other guests could burst into tears of sympathy, the bride clapped her hands. 'Footmen,

take this food away and feed it to the dogs!' she commanded. 'And, cook, fetch the other food—the dishes I told you to cook with salt.' Then she threw back her cloud-white veil, running the whole length of the table to kiss her father and show him her happy, shining face.

The Princess
and the Pea

Some people are hard to please and some even harder. When it came to choosing a wife, Prince Particular was hardest of them all. 'Unless I can find a Real princess,' he said, 'I shall not marry at all.'

'A royal princess, don't you mean?' said his mother the queen.

'Not at all. A Real princess is what I said and a Real princess is what I meant. These days there are imitations everywhere—girls passing themselves off, girls giving themselves airs, girls stre-e-etching the truth.'

'But you would never marry such a one!' said the queen.

'Never!' agreed the prince, and went in search of his dream. He scoured the land. He placed advertisements in the newspapers:

WANTED:
a Real Princess with a view to marriage.
Genuine applicants only please.

He met countless girls and numberless women. He danced till his shoes and his conversation wore out. But though he met Princess Rose and Maharanee Myrtle, Infanta Flora, Sultana Sunflower, and Tsarina

Tulip—and all of them claimed to be Real—Prince Particular was not satisfied with any of them. Women smiled at him from behind veils, from behind fans, from behind masks. But Prince Particular did not smile back.

By the time he arrived home he was travel sick and sick of travel, heartsick and sick of seeking someone to whom he could give his heart. He abandoned all hope of marrying. It seemed there was not a Real princess left in the entire world. Like the dodo, they had all become extinct.

One stormy winter night, as draughts set all the castle doors banging and the tapestries riffled against the walls, and the rugs lifted along the floor, there came a knocking at the door.

'Who's there?' called the king through the grille.

'A traveller in need of shelter, sir! Princess Verity is my name. The storm frightened my horses and I fell from my carriage, and I am a stranger in these parts. I have walked many miles through this storm, and I am very cold and hungry!'

The king squinted through the grille. The girl outside did not look much like a princess. Her clothes were muddy and torn, her hair bedraggled and her face pinched with cold. But she was pretty and well spoken . . . and anyway the king would not have left a dog out on such a night. So he let her in to drip puddles on the hall floor.

'A princess, eh?' said Prince Particular with a smug, knowing look.

'A princess, eh?' said the queen. 'We shall see.'

The waif perched at the table and ate dinner in tiny morsels off the tip of her fork. She spoke of palaces and protocol, of archduke uncles and dowager aunts, of art and music and poetry. The prince's mouth fell wider and wider open as he watched the fork and the mouth into which it disappeared. He actually found himself wanting to believe. He found himself believing . . . Could this be? Could this storm-sodden urchin possibly be a Real princess?

The queen knew how to find out. 'We shall soon see,' she whispered to her son. 'There is one sure way of knowing.' To Verity she said, 'You must be tired out, child. I shall go and prepare a bed for you.'

The queen went upstairs and removed from the guest bed both eiderdown and mattress. On the base of the bed she laid a single dried pea. Then she put back the mattress, and the eiderdown too. On top she placed another mattress and another eiderdown. On top of that a third. In fact she went on piling mattresses and quilts on top of one another till the bed reached almost to the ceiling—a great sagging mountain of goose feathers. A ladder had to be

fetched before 'Princess' Verity could even climb into bed.

At breakfast next morning, Prince Particular found himself looking forward very much to seeing Verity again. He almost wished his mother had not set a test for her. He wished he knew what the test had been.

When Verity appeared, she had washed, and her hair was combed and she did not drip on the floor. But she looked almost as pale as she had the night before, with dark circles under her eyes and no colour in her cheeks.

'I hope you slept well, my dear?' asked the queen, inspecting the girl through a pair of spectacles on a stick.

Verity smiled wanly and curtsied, sitting down at table as if the seats were a little too hard. 'Thank you,' she said.

'Well, did you or didn't you?' asked the queen (rather rudely, Particular thought). 'Did you sleep well?'

Verity ducked her head. 'Quite well,' she said.

'Aha! I knew it!' exclaimed the queen, banging the table in a way that startled the footmen. 'Throw her out, the imposter!'

The footmen blinked, coughed awkwardly and shuffled their feet. The queen called out the guard. The soldiers came running with pikes and pistols and swords and cords. But as they laid hands on the poor girl, she cried, 'Oh, please don't grip me tightly, gentlemen. I am black and blue all over with bruises. Something in my bed . . .'

'Wait!' said the queen imperiously. 'Unhand her! What was that you said, girl?'

Verity blushed to the roots of her golden hair. 'Oh dear. You will think me dreadfully ungracious, after all your kindness. My dear mother the queen always taught me, a guest should never complain. It's just that in my bed . . .'

'Yes?'

'Last night . . .'

'Yes?'

'There seemed to be a . . .'

'Yes?'

'Something small and hard. I just couldn't sleep at all!'

Much to Verity's surprise, the queen whooped with joy and kissed the king. The king kissed the footman—and the prince kissed Verity.

'Only a princess is made of such delicate stuff that she can feel a pea through twenty mattresses!' cried the queen. 'My apologies, princess! But now I know that you are truly a Real princess!'

'That's just as well,' said Prince Particular under his breath. 'I was going to marry her anyway.'